The Polygamist

Sue Nyathi

First published in South Africa by Logogog Press, 2012

Logogog Press
PO Box 44923
Claremont
7708
Cape Town
South Africa
www.logogog.com

ISBN 978-0-620-52260-1

Typeset by Logogog.
Cover design by Logogog.
Cover illustration: Lynda Ward.
Printed and bound by Interpak.
Designer: Marina Mentz
Project manager and editor: Paula Marais

The Polygamist

To

My Mother,
you inspire me to do better
and,
My Father
for not being a polygamist.

acknowledgements

My sincere gratitude goes to Paula Marais, my editor and publisher. Thanks to you and your team for breathing life into this baby.

And to Victor Utedzi, my partner in “crime”. Thank you for investing in this dream.

To my “girlfriends”, Terry Mafu, Jessica Manatsa and Precious Lwanga. Thank you for swallowing mouthfuls of *The Polygamist* from its inception to its final conclusion. Your constant cries for the next chapter ensured I kept writing and plotting till the end.

And to Nqobile Constance Githinji (1975–2011), my mentor. For always encouraging me to write...even when I didn’t want to write no more!

To my siblings Nduna, Kwanele and Minenhle. Thank you for your unfailing love and support.

And finally, to those men and women I did not mention by name but you know who you are. I thank each of you profoundly for sharing this journey with me.

prologue

Their eyes fell on his dull lifeless face. His features were contorted and his mouth twisted in a lopsided grin. The skin on his face was dry and crisp like burnt bacon. Even the fine smooth dark chocolate complexion he once boasted was now a darker shade of purple. The embalmer had done nothing to restore him to his former glory. He would have needed a sangoma to transform him to a fraction of his former self. He lay there, in swathes of white silk, his hands stiffly by his sides; none would have believed that this was a man who made women wet with one lustful look. Now he only brought shock and horror to the faces of the hundreds of mourners that had gathered inside the cold, grey, imposing enclave of the Catholic church. Each person had a different reason for being there. Some had genuinely come to pay their last respects. Others had come to make sure he was really dead.

A man of style, he would have been proud of the casket they had picked for him. No, the casket she had handpicked for him. It was made of pure mahogany and the glossy exterior shone in the brilliant light of the church. Given a choice she would have cremated him and scattered his ashes in the sewer but she had to keep up the charade to the end. She was glad he was dead. Glad that he would not wake up and cause her any more pain. How she had loved this man. How she had hated him too. At least now that he was gone, none of them could have him. She exhaled deeply. The truth was she lost him a long time ago. Even the love she once felt for him had died long before he did. She gave him one last look before walking away, head held up, her arm firmly entwined with that of their oldest son who almost disappeared under her tented black hat.

The tears rolled down her beautifully chiselled face. Huge perfectly formed droplets that would not stain her waterproof mascara. This was not the man she had once loved and coveted. What had become of him, her strong powerful handsome paramour? She had not been at his bedside when he died. If she had been, she might have killed him quickly and spared him the misery of a long protracted illness. They had many good memories together. Memories that were soured one fateful evening when he showed her another side of him she had never dreamed existed. With her lace handkerchief she obliterated another tear that rolled down her face. Her dark red cherry lips mouthed a goodbye. Something she had conveniently not done when she literally ran out his life a few years earlier.

Jonasi looked pitiful and sad lying there. She wanted to laugh. Even he would have hated himself had he woken up to see what had become of him. She almost felt sorry for him. Her sugar pie. Her caramel-covered doughnut. He was not a bad man, just a greedy one with such an insatiable appetite for sex. He had always boasted he could keep it going on for hours. Towards the end things had been difficult though. He had wilted like a flaccid erection. Poor man. At least now he had found peace in death. He had been in pain those last days. How she had longed to have been by his side, to give him comfort. However Joyce would not let them get close. She wanted him to all herself. Stupid bitch. She leaned down and kissed him one last time then walked out.

She gawked at him from behind her Gucci sunglasses. He looked terrible. How badly he had deteriorated towards the end. He had started to rot before her eyes. All the charm and charisma had disappeared when he had started to defecate on himself. She had been glad when Joyce had finally come to take his decaying body away. After that she had avoided him like a bad curse. Would she too look like the aftermath of a Haitian earthquake? Like him, robbed of her beauty and splendour as she was ravaged with illness? She shook her head in disdain. Her perfectly coiffed hair bounced around. This was not her fate. Jonasi might have been sapped of life but her whole life lay ahead of her with a myriad possibilities. Young and beautiful as she was, she was certain she would marry again. She stepped away from the casket, swinging her hips from side to side. Her Aldo heels clicked on the tiled floor. She had deliberately worn a body-hugging little black dress, showing off her legs to her fullest advantage. There were many rich sharks that had come to pay their last respects. Many who would not mind comforting his young, vulnerable widow. As she sashayed past the coffin, her eyes met with those of a handsome well-dressed man near the front pews. A jolt of electricity ran through her and she felt alive and energised. Good riddance to the dead; she had a lot of life in her and was going to live it to the full.

one

I am usually good at concealing my innermost emotions. But even I could not hide my disgust when my daughter announced she was getting married. She searched my face, looking for at least one wrinkle of approval. She found none.

"Why in hell do you want to get married?" I asked, "Are you in competition with your father?"

She stared at me, taken aback, "How can you even say that Mum? How can you even compare me to that moron?"

"He's your father," I replied pointedly.

"And your husband," she responded tartly.

Four wives later and yes I was still married to Jonasi Gomora. I don't know if I was fortunate or unfortunate to be wife number one. I guess it depends which way you look at it. Anyway the point is I can say with certainty that I was his first wife. I doubt others could say with certainty they would be his last. At 44 my husband was still hurtling along like a rolling stone. He had recently added another wife to the harem. Our own modern version of King Solomon. His latest acquisition had made a rather dramatic exhibition of herself at my daughter's 21st birthday. (My son could tell you more about that.) Anyway my husband likes them young. I had only been 16 when I met him. He had been 21 so it had not been so bad. How did anyone explain an age gap of almost three decades?

"I'm sorry Rudo. If you want to get married I can't stop you," I replied flippantly.

"Mum I want you to be happy for me," she replied.

"How can I? Marriage is just bullshit!"

"Mum it's not every marriage that is bullshit. There are happy couples out there. There are good men out there. Trevor is good. Trevor is a God-fearing man..."

I rolled my eyes heavenwards as she went on and on listing the merits of Trevor Sithole, the love of her life. Everyone finds some sort of escapism from an unhappy home. For my daughter it was religion. When she was old enough to realise what an asshole her father was she turned to God. I promise you it's due to God's grace that we are all alive to tell this story.

"Rudo, if this is what you want, my darling, you have my blessing."

"Mum do you really mean that?"

"I do," I replied, reaching out my hands to her and embracing her.

I faked it. I had to. This was my life now, faking the funk. Fake smiles, fake hair, fake nails... *I* even had problems wondering what was real anymore! Don't get me wrong. I love my daughter. I love her very much. I just want her to be happy but I'm not sure if she'll find the kind of happiness she wants in marriage. Especially not marriage to a black man. My sister is married to a white man and after thirty years she can still stand up and say they are happily married. Her husband always jokes that one wife is stressful enough! Why on earth would he want three? Maybe it's a status symbol for Jonasi, accumulating wives like he accumulates investments. It's true that gluttony is a sin and my husband is greed personified.

When I first met Jonasi he had nothing. N.O.T.H.I.N.G. My mother beat me when I announced that I wanted to get married to him, but there was nothing she could do about it. I was already four months' pregnant. This was considered to be the height of shame in my family. You see we were considered to be Zimbabwean royalty. My father was from the heart of Masvingo, and we could trace our ancestry to Great Zimbabwe. He had fled from what was called Rhodesia to study abroad. My father, being politically connected, served in several posts in the ZANU PF cabinet. Like many ministers' families we lived a life in the lap of luxury. I had everything I could possibly want or so I thought until I met Jonasi. I was hanging out at the shopping centre in Mount Pleasant waiting for my driver when he showed up. He was with three of his friends, but they paled in comparison. That was Jonasi for you. He stood out in a crowd. Jonasi was captivating with his handsome looks; there was no way you could ignore him. I had never seen anything like him before. Right there and then I thought Blair Underwood had stepped out of *L.A. Law* and into my life. He was in his first year of university then, studying finance and accounting. We chatted and he bought me an ice cream. I could tell he too was smitten. I'm a looker too you know. I inherited my looks from my mother. God forbid if I had turned out anything like my father. He resembles that bird on the Zimbabwean flag and with skin darker than midnight. I always used to wonder what Mama ever saw in him. I guess she also wondered what I saw in Jonasi. Our love blossomed, fanned by our all-consuming desire for each other. It was not long before I found myself writhing beneath his muscled body in the tiny cot bed of his smelly dormitory on the University of Zimbabwe campus. He took my virginity, right there on that bed. The springs almost gave way because we used to make love like dogs in heat. It's no surprise I fell pregnant. We were married quickly. If there was anything my dad abhorred it was scandal. When Dad walked me down the aisle, I hid my face behind the white veil of dishonour. Shortly afterwards, my father offered Jonasi a job at one of his many companies. He refused (and I loved him more for it). You see, long before anyone else did, I realised that Jonasi had potential: lots of it. I knew he was going to make it. I had faith in him then. Our first home was a one-roomed cottage in Queensdale. Look, I know I had fallen from grace but I told Jonasi I would never live in the location. After Independence, my father had taken us out of Highfields into the suburbs. That was progress; taking me back into the location would have been regression. Jonasi dropped out of university and got a job so that he could support me. He continued his studies with UNISA, studying well into the night. He would always creep into bed after midnight and still have energy to make love to me. We were happy in that one-roomed home. You have no idea how happy we were. No one believes it when I tell them that those were probably the happiest days in my married life. I never thought I could be happier and I never have been. Nothing will ever surpass those days. Jonasi graduated with honours, top of his class. I was there to witness the occasion with our three-year-old son, Tinotenda. My tummy was already bulging with our second child. Even before his graduation Jonasi had already received several job offers. He settled for one with a top accounting firm in Harare. Our fortune changed too as we now moved into a two-bedroomed flat in the Avenues. We also bought a car. I remember that Mazda 323 fondly. On weekends Jonasi would drive me and Tino to Avondale for ice cream. Such tiny little pleasures we take for granted. Rudo was born the following year and by the time our third baby Garikai came we were living in a house in the suburbs; a house much bigger than the one I grew up in. I made sure to remind my mother of this fact every time we met and she would goad me by saying my husband was ghetto fabulous. He was fabulous and rose through the ranks. He studied hard too and started to do his MBA. Then one day he told me he wanted to start his own company. He said he wanted to go into banking. Although I knew little how this fitted in the grand scheme of things I rallied behind him completely. If there was a trophy for cheerleading I would have won it because I was my husband's biggest supporter. I would have put the likes of Border Gezi to shame with my constant rallying. All that was left was for me to do was to get kitted out in java print regalia with Jonasi's face imprinted on it. I tell you, the things we do when we are young and naive.

"Mum are you listening?"

It was Rudo's sharp voice that brought me back to the present.

"Yes honey, you were saying?"

"So I'm going to go to *Tete* and tell her that Trevor wants to marry me!"

"Yes you must," I replied.

I suddenly got excited at the prospect of having to plan my daughter's wedding. If there's anything I do well it's throw a great party. I wondered where Rudo wanted to get married? We could have an exclusive do at home. The twins could be her little bridesmaids. They would look so gorgeous in their frocks. Shumi was too old to be a pageboy. I wondered if Rudo would include Sarah as a bridesmaid. She might have been older but she was still her sister. Knowing my daughter with her gigantic forgiving heart, anything was possible.

"Mum when did things start to go bad between you and Dad?"

"Is that a trick question?" I retorted.

"No seriously Mum. Things couldn't have always been this bad."

I exhaled deeply and mulled over that statement. The truth was things were never bad between us. Look every marriage has its ups and downs but we were coasting along just fine. Or maybe that was the problem, that things were just fine. I can't really pinpoint the exact moment when things got bad but what I can say is that things started to change the day I gave birth.

two

August 19, 2000. That was the day Shumirai was born. It was also the day Jonasi's company: J&J Holdings went from a private to public company with a riotous listing on the Zimbabwe Stock Exchange. The stock was over-subscribed ten times. That's what you call good fortune. I watched the short snippet on ZBC from my hospital bed. Jonasi was beside me and beside himself with joy. Even though I was drowsy from the anaesthetic I clanked my glass of orange juice against his tall glass of champagne in celebration.

"We are rich Joycie. We are fucking rich!" he exclaimed. He kissed me over and over again.

"I love you Joycie. You've done it again!"

"No sweetie," I replied, "You've done it again!"

I had no comprehension of just how rich we had become until when I was discharged from hospital there was a gleaming gold Mercedes C-Class parked outside with a big pink ribbon on the bonnet. Jonasi declared it was mine. It had personalised number plates: JOY 001. I laughed so much I was almost scared my stitches would come undone. He drove me whilst I sat in the backseat cradling Shumi in my lap. I was further promoted to a house in the hills in the posh suburb of Glen Lorne. Jonasi declared that with our newfound status we could still not be hanging around in the suburbs of Borrowdale. When I was implanted in a towering mansion in the exclusive Folyjon Crescent I had no doubt in my mind that we had arrived. In between nursing my new baby I was working with three interior designers from South Africa to get the house looking like Jonasi's personal kingdom. I literally threw myself into the world of drapes, cushions and Iranian carpets; mulled about the merits and demerits of Indonesian furniture versus Brazilian. This was my career, to be Jonasi's wife, lover and mother of his children. The best job in the world: with perks like these who could complain?

When Shumi turned one, I threw him a huge birthday party out in the beautifully groomed gardens surrounding our home. If I can say so, it was one party many mothers wanted to gatecrash. I hired a jumping castle, a clown to entertain the kids and had a horse too for the older children who wanted to be taken for a ride around our palatial home's garden. The mothers drank red wine and gossiped all afternoon. The only thing that marred that day was Jonasi's glaring absence when Shumi was coaxed to blow out his lone candle. Jonasi had been in attendance at all our children's birthdays. I had pictures to show for it. Now I tried to mask my discontent as I was pictured alone with my son. After the brouhaha of singing happy birthday had died down I went inside the house and called him again. His number was still unavailable. I exhaled deeply. He had left that morning to go play golf. I had reminded him not to be late for Shumi's birthday party. At the time, he said he would not miss it for the world and now it was close to 4 p.m. and he was still not back.

"Hey baby. I hope you are alright. We had to blow out the candles without you because it was getting late. Mwah. I love you."

I hung up and rejoined the party outside. It was starting to get rather chilly so I declared it was time to wrap things up. By 6 p.m. the house was deserted and the gardeners were cleaning up the mess. I was upstairs giving Shumi a bath and Rudo was my able assistant. She was a sweet, pliable 13 year old on the verge of puberty. In the family TV lounge on the same floor I could hear Tino fighting with Gari over the remote control. I knew Tino had won the fight when I heard Gari break out into a loud wail. He came into my bedroom crying.

"Mummy!" he wailed, "Tino won't let me watch my cartoons."

"Sweetie let him watch the TV. Remember he doesn't get to watch TV at school."

"He should go back to school. I hate it when Tino is around!"

At sixteen, Tino was a gangly pimpled teenager beset by mood swings. Garikai, who was eight years younger, irritated the hell out of him.

"Do you want to help me wash the baby?" I asked

"No," he replied, "that's girl stuff. I'm going to watch TV with Tino."

I lifted Shumi out of the water. I cooed at him lovingly and he cooed back. He had really enjoyed himself today. My darling little Shumi. After he was dressed I plugged him onto my nipple. He suckled greedily. Shumi fell asleep on my breast. He had been tired from the day's festivities. Children were lovely at this age. They did not throw tantrums, whine or fight. They were just bliss. I put him to sleep in his cot bed and went to supervise dinner. Even though I had two full-time maids, Jonasi still insisted I cook his supper. That night as I cooked, my eyes were transfixed on the driveway, hoping his Mercedes ML would come speeding into view. The children ate and went to bed and he was still not home. I fell asleep and was woken up by Shumi's screams for his midnight feed. Then I called him again. He was still unreachable. Now I was worried. It was unlike Jonasi to come home after midnight on a weekend. He could go drinking but he always knew to come home before midnight because my shop closed at 10 p.m. and after that he knew he could not get any until we opened for trading at 6 a.m. the next morning. It was our little joke. If I was having my period I would whisper in his ear and say, "Joyce General Dealer is closed for the holidays. Trading will resume in a week." Then after I had given birth he would turn to me and say, "Trading at Joyce General Dealers will be suspended until further notice." We had our own little thing going. After 16 years of marriage how could we possibly not? My heart constricted then at the thought of ever losing him. I reached for my cell phone and called him again. This time he answered.

"I'm on my way," he replied in a clipped voice.

Relief washed over me. I hung up, feeling slightly appeased. At least he was alright. The last thing I wanted was to lose him. I loved Jonasi with every nerve in my body. By the time he got home I had already put Shumi back to bed and was eagerly waiting up in bed for him. Many women say they tire of having sex with their husbands. I didn't. I wanted to ride my man. Ride him into the sunset. I craved Jonasi like he was a drug. He still did it for me, in every way.

"Sorry I missed out on the party," he declared as he walked through the door.

He threw a huge gift-wrapped box onto the bed.

"What happened Jona?"

He held up his hands in resignation, "It's a long story. Where's my boy?"

"Sleeping," I replied.

"I'll see him in the morning," he replied climbing into bed.

He gave me a hurried kiss and turned away from me. I curled into him, pressing my back into him. The scent on his body filled my nostrils. The mark of another woman imprinted on him.

"I'm tired Joyce."

I turned away from him. The perfume now permeated my own body and almost choked my insides. The tears rolled down my cheeks. I bit down on my tongue to stop myself from crying out loud. I know you might think I'm naive but I had never ever questioned my husband's fidelity. I promise you, it's something that never crossed my mind. Jonasi had never given me any reason to think he would ever cheat on me, until that night.

I woke up in the morning and wore a sunny smile and told myself everything was going to be alright. I got dressed and made sure the kids were ready for church. When we left, Jonasi was still sleeping. Every Sunday was the same in our home. I took the kids to church and Jonasi would recover from his Saturday-night hangover. When we came home we would have a family braai. Sunday was "our" day. However when I came home from church and did not find Jonasi's car lodged in the driveway my insides lurched. I knew then, that everything was wrong, so very wrong. He had left a note to say he had to rush to work and would make it up to me. I crunched up that note and threw it against the wall. That afternoon I held the braai tongs and burned the meat and boerewors whilst the children splashed around the pool making a loud noise. I drank too much and got so inebriated. Then I started laughing at everything so much that I cried. At some point I passed out and it was Jonasi who woke me up. He was shouting at me. At first I could not hear him then slowly his words became audible.

"...Irresponsible. How can you get drunk when you are nursing? Shumi's been crying his lungs out and you couldn't hear him?"

"You heard him, why didn't you quiet him? He's your son too."

"You're his mother!" he shouted back, "It's your responsibility."

I stood up and like a zombie walked towards Shumi's cradle. His bum was soaking wet. He just needed a nappy change.

"Why didn't you change him Jona? The nappies are in your face!" I shouted back, "You didn't want to get your hands dirty? No that's Joyce's job isn't it?"

"Shut up Joyce. You're drunk!"

"Shut up Joyce. You're drunk," I mimicked after him.

He glared at me, annoyed more than ever. I started to laugh. He looked so serious. Why was he so serious?

"It's late," I said, "Where are you coming from? Work?"

"Somebody has to make the money around here. You think if I didn't go to work you'd be living in this house or driving that Merc? No Joyce, you would be out on the streets crawling on your fat ass."

I looked at my ass. When had it become fat? I thought he liked my fat ass.

"I'm going to sleep in the spare bedroom," he said, "I'm not in the mood for your shit!"

He walked off. He slammed the door behind him. My heart thumped. I crawled into bed with Shumi. I cried. Shumi woke up and started crying. We both cried until we fell asleep. When the tears start pouring down, you know shit has hit the fan! I knew then that this was the beginning of the end.

three

I lay on my side and watched him breathing in his sleep. I was totally enamoured with the man who lay asleep beside me. I had never seen anything so beautiful in my life. He was perfect; every feature on his face was perfect. Just to wake up beside him gave me a rush. This was something I could get very used to. He opened his eyes and caught me staring at him. I smiled and he smiled too. The heavens could have opened and swallowed me that morning. It was one of those moments you would have loved to capture on camera but could not. There had been a lot of those "moments" lately; too many actually. I was starting to think I would lose count of them.

"Good morning Joey," I crooned then leaned over to kiss him lovingly.

"Morning legal eagle," he replied.

That was his pet name for me.

"You did some illegal things to me last night," he cajoled as he began drawing circles on my back with his fingers.

I giggled, "You were caught with your pants down so you had to be arrested."

The handcuffs that were attached to the four-poster bed gleamed in the early morning light. I got goose pimples as I thought of what had transpired the night before. The sex between us had always been explosive. I always knew it would be. Sparks flew the day I first met Jonasi Gomora. It was at one of those high-powered corporate functions. We did not talk or anything but we exchanged one look and I just knew. The second time I met Jonasi was in an oak-panelled boardroom on the tenth floor of J&J Holdings on Union Avenue. I was there for an interview for the post of Legal and Compliance Affairs Manager, Investment Banking. Every self-respecting person in Harare wanted to work for J&J Holdings. It was the most successful black-run business in the city. And here I was sitting face to face with one of the most respected CEOs in the game. The other members of the panel were the Human Resources Director, the Director of Investment Banking, the Director of Legal Affairs and Compliance and of course Mr Man himself. There was only one woman on the panel and I could tell she hated me on sight. I elicit that kind of reaction in most women. They are threatened by me. Look I am no beauty queen, far from it actually, but I make the most of what I have. Ever heard of making a dollar go the whole damn mile, that's me. If I were put in a room full of Miss Worlds I would not go unnoticed, that I can assure you. Needless to say I got the job. There were three other candidates, but I had no doubt in my mind that I would be the one they would choose. When I see something I want I go for it and make sure I get it. I don't believe in that adage that "when you lose something it was never meant for you." Shit, when you lose something it's because you didn't fight hard enough to get it. As I stood outside the imposing J&J Holdings building I told myself this job was mine and God help anyone who would stand in my way. I started right away. I had managed to get myself an over-the-top package because I negotiated well. I know my worth and I know I'm good at what I do. At least I give off that impression so I might as well be paid for it. I could see the Human Resources lady baulk when I mentioned that I wanted a starting salary of 40K, non-negotiable. She was quick to point out that for that position it was too much.

I was not fazed. "I won't leave my present job for any less," I stated flatly.

In the corner of my eye I could see Jonasi smile. You see it's only fair. I spent four years in university reading law, then another two years doing a Masters. Then people want to pay you slave wages, hell no! I got a dingy little office on the fifth floor with all the other juniors on my level. Yet my heart yearned to be on the tenth floor with the rest of the bigwigs of the company. I felt like I had been relegated to the back of the bus. Who was going to see me here? Certainly not Jonasi. My power suits and high-heeled shoes were wasted on the little boys who were panting after me in the corridors of J&J Holdings. Power, money and sex are the biggest aphrodisiacs in life and in that order. You can't have one without the other. That's the problem with guys my age. They can only offer you one and a half and power doesn't even come into the equation! So I made up my mind I was going to work my way up to be recognised. And you won't believe my luck; a few months after joining J&J; the CEO announced that they were making plans to list on the Zimbabwe Stock Exchange. This transaction kept us awake day and night. I didn't mind. I love a challenge and what was nice was that we worked closely with Jonasi. He wasn't one of those CEOs who just delegated work and then oversaw the results. He was hands on. We would be up until 2 a.m. and he would be there too. Wide awake and alert. The man was tireless, a fountain of energy. Stories had also done the rounds that he was tireless in bed and had a voracious sexual appetite. Rumour had it that his personal assistant also doubled up as his personal sex slave during lunch hours. The way she was so possessive over him I would not put it past her. She was like a fortress around him. If I was not working on the team with him I doubt I would gotten a glimpse of him and I suspect many of the staff at J&J had not seen him. At J&J, you have the ground floor, which is where the commercial bank is. You walk in there and all the bank tellers look like they are former beauty queens. Grooming is a huge part of our work ethos. We actually get an allowance on our payslip for personal grooming. On the second floor you have the bankers. The third floor is dedicated to the micro-finance arm and on the fourth floor there is the stock-broking arm. The fifth floor, which is where I am, is where we have the investment and corporate banking divisions. I don't know who or what is on the other floors but I know that the big boss occupies the tenth floor. I had never been into his office until one evening as we were packing up he asked me to come through. It was a massive office, made up of a series of smaller rooms. There was the reception area in the front, a small lounge with a huge TV screen showing the activities on the world markets, a smaller boardroom and finally his office (it was only later I discovered the dressing room and bathroom behind that office).

"Take a seat," he said pointing to the leather armchair behind his desk.

I eased into it with confidence, crossing one leg over

another. I won't lie, I was trembling a bit. Jonasi is like that with people. He has a way of throwing them slightly off guard. I think it's because he is so tall and imposing. My eyes darted across the room, trying to absorb every detail. He had several pictures on the wall, several framed accolades. He had really done well for himself. On his huge desk he had pictures of his family. He caught me looking at one.

"That's my family," he pointed out, "And that's my wife," he said reaching for another gold-framed portrait.

I was curious to see what Mrs Jonasi Gomora looked like. I had never seen her before and she never came around to the office. Why would she when she saw the man at home every night? Truth be told, she was beautiful with long black beautiful hair, beautiful coffee-coloured skin and beautiful milky white teeth behind a beautiful smile. The perfect little beautiful family.

"She's beautiful," I remarked, "And so are the kids."

He smiled, "Thanks. But I didn't call you in here to make small talk about my family. I called you in here to commend you on your hard work and commitment to the company. I am really impressed."

"Thank you," I replied with my most winning smile.

He did not reciprocate, but just stared at me and then turned away and said, "That's all. You can go now."

I left his office thinking was that it? Had I been hoping that he would try pull a move on me? Or at least try and proposition me! Or maybe I just wasn't his type? Maybe he liked them light and bright like missy in that picture. I'm dark as a blueberry but I'm sweet like sherry! So I guess you are still wondering how I got Jonasi under my skin. Well it actually happened on the day J&J listed. We had this huge celebration in the boardroom (for the top floor guys but I was invited). He left midway because his wife had gone into labour. When he returned hours later the party had invariably broken up. As he headed up to his office he met me in the elevator. He asked me to join him for a drink as he was still in a celebratory mood. How could I say no to the big boss? Trust me we had a few drinks in that big office of his. He opened a bottle of Johnny Walker Black and needless to say I started to see a side of my CEO I had never seen before. He said he wanted to make love to me on his desk, a long-nursed fantasy of his. Like the committed employee I am, I was quick to oblige him. He pushed me onto his desk, which sent the picture of Joyce flying off it. And that was how it all began.

four

I am not a violent person. Honest to God I am not. I even have trouble hitting the children. Jonasi was always the disciplinarian. I was the one the kids ran to after they had been smacked. So it came as a surprise to everyone, me included, when I attacked Matipa. You see it was one of those days, a nothing-out-of-the-ordinary kind of day when I was minding my own business as usual. I had just fed Shumi and put him to bed and was on my way to Borrowdale to pick up Gari from school. As I had an hour to kill I decided to do some shopping at Sam Levy's village. That's what you do when you have too much time and money on your hands. I went to Zuva, a classic designer shop that stocked a lot of original (and expensive) outfits. I had found a dress I liked and headed into the changing room when I overheard two girls in the other cubicle chatting at the top of their voices about Jonasi. Their conversation brought me to a skidding halt. You see there are not many men in Harare with a name like Jonasi so I was bound to take notice.

"Jonasi will love it. I'm sure his wife has never bothered

to wear anything like it!"

"Even if she wanted to she couldn't fit into it. Joyce should be swimming in Kariba with all the other hippos!"

There was loud raucous laughter, followed by, "Matipa you can be so cruel. The poor bitch has had four kids."

"She wanted to; no one forced her too. Jonasi tells me she even has stretch marks on her teeth. How disgusting can you get?"

That was when I opened the curtain to their dressing cubicle. Matipa was the one standing half dressed whilst her friend looked on in admiration. She had a long mane of fake hair that reached her waist. Kind of reminded me of Rapunzel. Except that she was a repulsive Rapunzel.

"Excuse me!" she said tartly, "I'm trying to get dressed."

She spoke with a condescending twang like she owned the damn fucking world. Well I was going to teach her a lesson. That's when I charged towards her like a raging bull. I grabbed her by the neck and pushed her into the mirror and banged her head hard against it. Her friend flew out of the cubicle. I'm not sure if this was to call for help or to get as far away from me as possible. I did not care either way. All I was worried about was to sort out this bitch in front of me. Suddenly all the anger that was inside me came bubbling over. I slapped her hard across the face. Once, twice, until I lost count. By the time the guard came to see what the fracas was about I had Matipa by the hair banging her face into the wall. The female guard held me from behind and tried to restrain me from inflicting further damage.

"Whore," I screamed, "If you want to sleep with my husband, do it quietly."

It did not take long for the short, stubby uniformed woman to realise that the woman lying on the floor in a heap was the cause of my angst. She released me and kicked Matipa in the face with the rounded mouth of her shiny boots. Matipa yelped out in pain.

"Shut up," hissed the guard. "If you scream again I'll break both your legs."

Then she kicked her again. I smiled in grim satisfaction.

Matipa re-emerged from the changing room, limping, and looking blue in the face. The guard had a firm hand around her skinny arms and all I could see were pain and fear in her big black eyes. Her friend had threatened to call the police on me.

"Call them," I said, "Go ahead and call them."

"Don't call!" mumbled Matipa in an almost inaudible voice "Let's just get out of here."

"We don't allow fighting in here, ladies," spoke the manageress.

"I can happily take it outside," I replied.

Matipa's friend wrapped her arm around her and helped her out of the shop. I stayed behind to thank the female guard.

"Any time mama. If ever you need a favour you can ask me. It's those kind of bitches that break up our homes."

Instead of buying the dress I gave the money to the guard and walked off feeling euphoric. I even played music on the radio loud. I could not remember feeling this happy in a while. I picked up Gari from school and decided to do a detour and see my mother. Jonasi called a couple of times in between. I ignored all his calls.

When I told my mother what had happened she merely looked at me and said it was long overdue. You see as much as my mother likes to act like she's got class, she's more ghetto fabulous than all of us put together. She was born and bred in Mbare and literally clawed her way out of there to where she is now and she's proud of it.

"Did you get that guard's number?"

"Whatever for Mama?"

"You need to finish her off. Beat her up in her own home and pretend some thieves broke in!"

I started to laugh, "You're not serious Mama."

"I am. You need to make sure you break both her legs. She thinks she can fuck your husband and go around shouting it at the top of her lungs. Break both those legs so that she can't fuck no more. Trust me; I once braised the skin off a bitch's back."

I laughed until I had tears running down my face.

"I did," replied my mother in earnest, "I poured boiling water down her back. She spent six months in hospital lying on her tummy. I made sure she wouldn't be fucking anyone in a long time! You know, Joyce, you have to put your foot down. You can't have little bitches who think they own the world saying bullshit about you. You are Mrs Gomora; they should respect you."

"How can they when my own husband doesn't!"

"Oh come now, don't be naive. You think if Jonasi tells them you are a wonderful woman they will pull them panties down? They won't. Now here's what you should do Joyce. Play it cool. "

I drank down my mother's advice like a warm cup of tea with sugar and cream. That evening when I got home I was surprised to see Jonasi's car lodged in the driveway. I found him pacing the bedroom like an agitated bull. For a minute I thought he would beat the living daylights out of me but I shoved the thought aside. Jonasi had never once laid a hand on me.

"Joyce," he began, "I'm very disturbed by your behaviour."

My behaviour? If there was anyone with disturbing

behaviour it was him. Who had stopped coming home at night? Who had started being away from home days at a time and not even for business trips but pure unadulterated pleasure? Even when he played with the kids on weekends he was distracted and you could tell he could not wait to get away from them. From us. We were no longer the family he lived for. Rather we were the noose around his neck.

"What do you mean, Jonasi?"

"Since when do you go around mauling innocent people in shopping malls?"

I stifled a laugh, "Come on Jonasi, do I look like I could hurt anyone? Who was I supposed to have injured?"

"Joyce it's not funny. Matipa had to be hospitalised. She is also traumatised."

"And I'm not Jonasi? You think what you are doing to us has not traumatised me? Why can't you stop being selfish!"

"You are the selfish one Joyce. You have everything here. Why can't you be happy? Why?"

I looked at him and realised it was not Matipa who needed the hiding it was him. I was going to go back to Sam Levy's and have that guard organise a squad of men to beat Jonasi to a pulp and leave him lying for dead. Now I understood why women had their husband's murdered. It was for things like this.

"Joyce, are you even listening to me?" he asked.

"I am," I replied.

"I said I want a divorce. I love Matipa and I want to be with her."

I sat on the bed, feeling heady and light. I felt like the air had gone out of me. As if someone had stuck a pin in my side. He came and sat beside me. He took my hand in his and held it for a long time; my hand that was adorned with gold rings that I had acquired through our marriage. A marriage that Jonasi was ready to dissolve for the black bitch I had beaten to a pulp. She wasn't even pretty. Sure, she had a great body, but so did I before I had the four kids. It was not fair. How could he want to destroy our marriage over a fleeting affair? It would burn out and Jonasi would come to his senses.

"Joyce you are my first love and you will always be. I love the children and I will continue to take care of you. You can have anything you want."

Yes I could have everything I wanted except Jonasi. How could that be when not so long ago I had everything I wanted *and* Jonasi. Did he not understand how much I loved him? I had left my parents' home because of him. Everything I had done in my life was for this man. I started to cry then. Why?

He put his arm around me, "Joyce we can still be friends. You and I have always been good friends. I will always provide for you and the kids. Anything you want you will always have Joyce. That I promise you."

He kissed me on the cheek and then left. He was gone for the whole week. Probably nursing Matipa. I suddenly wished I had killed her. I wanted to kill myself then but Shumi's cries in the background reminded me that my children needed me. Jonasi might not need me but what would happen to them? So I chose to live and I cried instead. I was totally inconsolable. In the end, Tino resorted to calling my mother; I guess because he tried to call his father and could not get hold of him. My mother was the one who got me out of bed and up and running again.

"We don't fall apart Joyce," she said with her usual efficacy, "We get even."

"Mama I don't want another man," I said.

"I didn't say get another man," she replied, "Just get even. Jonasi is an ass if he thinks he can just walk out of here and leave you with four kids. You should have told him to take the kids with him. Trust me that bitch would not want him then."

"Mama I couldn't do that to my kids," I wailed.

She stared at me, "I know. That's the problem."

"Would you have left us if Dad had decided to walk out on you?"

"The thing is your father would never have dreamed of walking out on me Joyce. I'm not saying your father was a saint. As ugly as he was, he still had whores trailing after his ass. But he knew I would not take that kind of bullshit. In all the time we were married, your father never once slept outside our home unless he was at some Zanu PF rally. He knew not to mess with me and tell me some bullshit about a divorce. Your problem is that you've given Jonasi free reign here. He thinks he can literally walk all over you. It's not fair, my darling. We don't go out like that. You've given that man your whole life, Joyce. You deserve better than this. Jonasi might have made the money but you supported him every inch of the way. You polished him up and gave him class. Don't think for a minute you didn't contribute because you did. So he divorces you and gives you a measly 10 percent and some good-for-nothing cow is going to enjoy the 90 percent. No Joyce, that's just not right. If he wants to divorce you, he'll do it over your dead body. You are not going to sign any divorce papers, my baby. You are going to hang in there until that cow goes blue in the face and we'll see what happens then. Like I said before, my baby, we don't fall apart, we get even."

So I decided then that that's what I would do.

five

The biggest mistake Joyce ever made was hitting me. I played the role of the victim so well that I had Jonasi eating out of my pussy. It was not long either before Jonasi had literally moved in with me. Not long before he was singing the "divorce" chorus at the top of his lungs. I told you before; I go for the jugular vein. I don't fight with my hands but I fight with my head. That's the attraction between Jonasi and me, we can stimulate each other mentally and then the sex just flows. Don't get me wrong, we are not always in the bedroom. We play golf together on hot summer afternoons and play chess near the fire on cold winter evenings. Sometimes I lie curled in his arms watching old episodes of *Carson's Law*. Our favourite ritual is Sunday-morning breakfast where we eat out on the patio and then we pore through pages and pages of newspapers. Even when he has pressing concerns at work he comes to me. Before long I was moved up to the ninth floor and my title changed to Assistant Director: Legal Compliance and Corporate Affairs. I was now responsible for overseeing the whole company and not just investment banking. A lot of people sniggered that I got promoted because I was shagging the CEO. Look I won't lie, shagging him helped moved things along but the bottom line is I am good at my job. I am good at what I do and if I had been at any other company they would have seen it too. Only difference is I might have had to wait till I was forty instead of thirty to get where I am now. I am very happy with a big office overlooking the city of Harare and just one floor separating him from me. His PA now pays attention to me because she knows who calls the shots. The power balance has really been shifted. I feel it when I walk in the corridors of J&J; even the other directors are wary of me. You see only employees at their level can get to drive an E-Class Mercedes Benz but I am also rolling in one now and no one can say a thing. I used to rent a penthouse in Northfields opposite the Harare Sports Club but for my thirtieth birthday Jonasi bought it for me and it's in my name. We practically live together now. He goes home every now and then to check on the kids but that's about it; he's with me now. He doesn't love Joyce and if she knew what was good for her she would sign the divorce papers and walk off with a fat settlement and everybody could get on with their lives. I also want to start planning my wedding you know.

"What are you doing?" asked Jonasi, slipping his arms around me.

"I'm just fixing you a sandwich before we head off to the golf club."

He kissed me on the side of the neck, "You are so thoughtful."

Just then the doorbell rang. I wondered who that could be; I was not expecting anyone. Neither was he. I went to answer the door and from the peephole I saw Joyce's face.

"It's your wife," I called out to Jonasi.

"I'll handle it," he said.

"No darling, let me," I replied, knowing full well I had the might of Jonasi behind me. What could she possibly do to me? She was on my turf now.

I opened the door and a fuming Joyce stood there staring back at me. She looked awful, with bags under her eyes. You know how you look when you haven't slept in days? Joyce was not an old woman, however she looked haggard. Worse, she had lost too much weight. I guess it was a combination of a hunger strike and not sleeping. Next she would be picketing outside my door. She had not come alone I saw. She'd brought the children to see for themselves the pig their father had shacked up with.

"Hello Joyce," I spoke sweetly.

She did not respond. Instead she walked passed me and straight into the living room where Jonasi was seated.

"I brought the kids for the weekend. If you and your missus think you can shack up in your love nest without any responsibilities you've got another thing coming."

"Joyce you are being unreasonable!" replied Jonasi. "Where do you think the children will play?"

"I don't know Jonasi; you make a plan."

She shoved the baby into his hands with instructions on his feeds and napping times.

"Have a good weekend. I'll pick them up on Sunday."

She turned and walked away before I could even say anything. Jonasi stood there in stunned silence.

He finally spoke, "I'm sorry about this."

I shrugged my shoulders, "It's alright."

It was not alright but what could I say exactly? No Jonasi, get your fucking kids out of my house? He then took me by the hand and introduced me to them. They were cold. The girl would not even look at me as she held onto her baby brother tightly. This was going to be even harder than I thought.

"Anyway we should get going," I suggested to Jonasi. "Come on guys."

Jonasi eyed me quizzically, "You want to bring them along to golf? They can stay home and watch TV."

I would not leave them in my house unattended. God only knows what they would do. They could easily run riot and break my vases and ornaments. Not to mention the mess they would create and who would clean up after them? Besides, how many children do you know who want to be left at home to watch television? I hated it when my parents would go out and leave us.

"Let's go with them. It's a beautiful day outside and they can play putt-putt or something."

So we all went to the country club together. I suggested Jonasi take the boys and teach them to play. Rudo, Shumi and I walked the course alongside the Gomora men. Actually I was quite surprised at how well behaved Shumi was. He did not cry at all unless he was hungry and then he would also want to toddle along on the green. After two hours of golf we went and had lunch at the country club. I could tell the older boys had enjoyed themselves immensely with their father. Their faces were flushed with happiness. It occurred to me then that Jonasi did not really spend quality time with his children. It was one thing to sit with your kids and quiz them about school and life but quite another to actually include them in your social life and do something fun with them. Joyce was probably the better parent, probably knew them better because she spent a lot more time with them.

"What now?" asked Jonasi after he'd paid the bill for lunch.

I could tell he was nervous. Edgy. He was so used to just offloading the children onto Joyce when he had tired of them.

"Let's go and watch a movie," I suggested.

The children agreed wholeheartedly with me and I knew then that this was going to be my trump card. Tino was a little reluctant about the movie business but Gari and Rudo were excited at the thought. I could already tell they did not get out much. Joyce kept them cosseted in that house like there was no world outside the four walls of their Folyjon home.

"And Shumi?" asked Jonasi.

"Shumi's just fine," I replied.

So we piled into their daddy's ML and drove off to the movie house in Avondale. We caught the 3 p.m. movie. One of those PGA movies, I forget the title. Shumi fell asleep in the dark and rested his head on my chest. For the first time in my life I thought I might actually want to have a baby of my own.

"Thank you for being so understanding," whispered Jonasi in my ear.

"Sweetheart," I replied, "I love you and your kids."

After the movie we had dinner at IBs. Then Jonasi decided we should check into the Holiday Inn Crowne Plaza because he did not want the children crowding my flat. Who was I to object? You think I relished the idea of having to wake up in the morning to cook breakfast for six? We slept with Shumi. Once he was fast asleep Jonasi and I made love. Afterwards he told me how much he loved me. I told him I loved him even more.

"I'm thinking," he said, "If we are going to have the kids

around we should get a bigger place."

My eyes lit up like diamonds. I liked the sound of that, a bigger place.

"Oh yes that would be great, something with eight bedrooms just in case I have our kids too."

"Matipa I'm serious. I want us to have a child together."

"We will Jonasi. I just want your children to get to know me better and then like me before we start having kids of our own. The last thing you want is for them to feel sidelined."

"I guess you're right," he replied. "God what would I do without you?"

"No Jonasi," I replied sweetly. "What would I do without you?"

We kissed and he held me tightly. The last thing I was going to do was have children with Jonasi. Especially seeing as the divorce papers had not even been signed yet. Look I'm in love with the man but trust me I haven't lost my head yet.

six

Of all my children, Rudo acted like it was my fault Jonasi had left us. You see she was her daddy's little girl and his absence from our lives hurt her too. She made me feel inadequate as a wife and mother. The day I dumped them over at their father's girlfriends' house I thought I was actually opening up Matipa's eyes to the baggage that came with Jonasi. I actually thought she would be so disgusted and run a mile. But what do you know; the bitch embraced my children wholeheartedly. She treated them like they were her own. At first I thought she was pretending but after a year, I knew she meant business. Even Rudo would sit there defending her, "She's not such a bad person Mum. She's actually nice." Only Tino stood by my side and told me that he thought Matipa was a whore. That he would always consider her a whore. At least I was assured of one ally in the family. Garikai blew like the wind. He loved you one minute and hated you the next. Even Shumi could not be counted on. The minute he could start talking he muttered "Mata, mata" instead of "mama". I still had not signed the divorce papers, but in reality I was just as good as divorced. Jonasi no longer set foot in my house. He now lived permanently with Matipa in a gigantic house in Ballantyne Park. I had never been there but Rudo told me it had six bedrooms and they had all been allocated a room. She said the décor was different, more modern and upmarket but insisted my house had understated glamour and class. So that made me smile. The younger children now visited their father every other weekend without fail. Tino refused to visit his father and preferred to spend his weekends with me when he was around from school. My loyal son; he was the only one who had my back. The only time he spoke to his father was when Jonasi came to drop off his siblings. Even then, the conversations were short and stilted. Tino made it very clear to Jonasi whose side he was on. However, that did very little to move him. The only thing that rocked his world now was Matipa's black ass. Matipa was also making an indelible impression on my children. The minute they got back on Sundays it would be Matipa this, Matipa that. It was always *Matipa lets us eat as much chocolate as we want. Matipa lets us stay up until midnight. Matipa does not force us to bath at night...* Of course I would listen with mounting bitterness. At one point I was on the verge of telling them to fuck off and stay with Matipa forever. Little ungrateful assholes. I carried them for nine months and they wanted to lay the law of Matipa in my house. I was just counting the days till Matipa got pregnant and had children of her own. She and Jonasi would become so besotted with the new children that mine would be shoved aside, completely ignored. That would teach them for betraying their mother. Some days I felt like I was actually rehearsing my life as a divorcée, that I was getting a sneak preview of my life without Jonasi. Actually there was a rumour going around that Jonasi and I were divorced. Who could blame them thinking that when Jonasi and Matipa were always seen together publicly? They were even pictured together in newspapers. The last time I opened the *Financial Gazette* I saw their smiling faces at the opening of a new banking branch in Gokwe. Matipa was cutting the ribbon and Jonasi stood beside her. I remember snorting and thinking didn't the bank have a PR person to do that sort of thing. So I rightly assumed when he travelled abroad, he packed her in his suitcase. I realised I was slowly fading into the background. Very soon no one would know who the real Mrs Gomora was. That was when I decided to throw a party. There is nothing like a good party to stir things up and this time I had a reason to celebrate; it was our seventeenth wedding anniversary in two months. Seventeen years is a long time to be married. Ask anyone; some people don't even get past the five-year mark. This was an achievement and I was going to celebrate it in style. The house was the perfect venue. Ever since we had moved in I had not actually had a chance to really show it off to any of our friends. That was because my life had been literally falling apart. No more of that. People needed to be reminded that there was only one Mrs Jonasi Gomora and she was here to stay. I had not come this far, after all these years so that I could retire gracefully from the race. Only in death would I be parted from Jonasi. He would have to kill me first if he thought I was going anywhere. Tino thought I was crazy when I started drawing up the guest list but I assured him I was going to pull it off. My mother came in to help. She also added to the list her collection of ZANU PF friends. What's a party if you can't get the bigwigs of Harare to come? Besides it would give it more clout. I hired the Meikles Hotel to do the catering. I decided to go the full monty with a five-course sit-down meal with a full bar. I even insisted they bake a miniature wedding cake with the number 17 on top. My father managed to get the full army brass band to entertain, and then of course I had the disco guys who would have people on their feet 'til the early hours of the morning. The colour theme for the party was burgundy and cream. I made sure this was reflected in the décor, the cards and the dress code. Then I mailed the invites three weeks before. Gold-lined invites on silky perfumed embossed paper.

JOYCE & JONASI GOMORA
cordially invite

……………………………….

to celebrate their seventeenth wedding anniversary
It's been seventeen fabulous years,
Come celebrate with us.
J&J

For good measure I even sent one to Matipa. Just to remind her that she was hallucinating if she thought she could bulldoze a 17-year marriage. I can just see you rolling your eyes thinking what a pathetic excuse I am for a woman. That if you were in my shoes you would have packed your bags and left a long time ago. The thing is that you are not in love with Jonasi. You did not have four kids with the man. You had not built a life with the man. I loved him and I was not ready to give up because I strongly believed that Matipa was a fleeting fancy that would soon blow over. Jonasi was going through a midlife crisis and I had faith that he would soon realise that I was the real deal. Even as I sealed those invites I still nursed the hope that Jonasi would come back home where he belonged. My darling husband was the first person to RSVP. I had made sure to hand deliver his invite personally. That day I dressed to the nines. I wore a white linen wrap dress that was just cut above the knees showing off my light legs. The gold chains around my neck glistened, and were almost swallowed by my gaping cleavage. I topped the ensemble off with my Chanel sunglasses. My hair was cut short and curled. I used to have long hair before I cut it off in a rage some time after Jonasi had decided to leave me. I have to say the short hair looks dramatic – even looking at my own reflection in the lift made me smile. I swung done the corridors in my gold espadrilles, the strings tied up to my knees, leaving a trail of Christian Dior's "Poison" behind me. The PAs on the tenth floor were all alarmed to see me. I almost told them to shut up and get on with it. Had they also forgotten I was the other J in J&J? Unfortunately Jonasi was in a meeting so I could not sit and wait to see his reaction when he opened the card, but trust me I heard his reaction when he called me later on in the day. He was stark raving mad.

"Joyce what are you playing at?" he barked.

"Nothing," I replied coyly, "It's our seventeenth wedding anniversary, and I want to celebrate it! Just like we've always done."

We had celebrated the last sixteen so why break with tradition? Sometimes it's best to stick with the tried and tested.

"What are you celebrating? We are not even together anymore!"

"We are. In my heart, we are still together."

Matthew chapter four, verse one was explicit: "For this reason a man will leave his father and mother and be united to his wife, and the two will become one flesh. So they are no longer two, but one. Therefore what God has joined together let no man put asunder."

"Get a grip Joyce! If you had any sense you would be signing the divorce papers. You and I have been over for a long time! I want to start making new memories now..."

I exhaled deeply and put my hand over the mouthpiece. There were some things I was better off not knowing. Things that he said that made my heart bleed. When I could not take any more I just cut him off abruptly.

"Listen here Jonasi, you are still my husband, whether you like it or not and we are going to celebrate our seventeenth-year wedding anniversary. The Minister of Finance is going to be here so make sure you are here too. I wouldn't want you to lose your banking licence over unnecessary things!"

I slammed the phone down so hard the room felt like it was reverberating with the tension. Tino was there, standing beside me. He hugged me. The tears were rolling down my face. And just like that I went from a conquering heroine to a blithering fool.

"Mummy you don't have to do this," he said quietly.

I was almost tempted to cancel the whole thing but I decided not to. Jonasi was not going to ruin my seventeenth-year wedding anniversary party.

And so as the day drew closer my anxiety mounted. The excitement was now gone and instead it was replaced with dread when I thought of the embarrassment I would suffer if Jonasi did not turn up. My mother told me not to worry about it and that she was certain Jonasi would show up. The day of the party she had me checked into the Clarins Beauty Spa. They scrubbed me inside out if that's possible. All the hairs on my body were plucked and trimmed into shape (including the pubic ones). Then they gave me a full body massage. I am even embarrassed to say this but I had an orgasm from the way the masseur was touching me. That's what happens when you go for too long without sex! Strangely my anxieties melted. That evening I was as radiant as a glow-worm. My mood was infectious as everyone around me was in a buoyant mood. Little Shumi was running wild with excitement proclaiming it was his party. I was scared he was going to mess himself. I had him decked out in a little suit. He looked so gorgeous he almost brought tears to my eyes. Jonasi did show up, looking debonair and elegant in a black tuxedo with a burgundy bow tie. He said I looked good and trust me I did. I wore a silk burgundy suit, matching shoes and a tiny hat with a little veil. Around my neck I wore some pearls Jonasi had brought me in Paris three years before for my thirtieth birthday. Jonasi was very affectionate and put his arms around me as we posed for the family portraits around the house with our sons kitted in shiny suits and my daughter in her burgundy taffeta dress. The night went beautifully. The guests arrived in all their finery. Jonasi and I received each of them with the fortitude of a couple that has been through some very rough times. I tell you, seeing us that night no one would have guessed we no longer lived in the same house. It was not just keeping up appearances though because through dinner we joked and laughed like old times. It was really nice and, yes, a couple of times Jonasi's hand strayed over to my thighs (and I welcomed it, he is my husband!). I might have said it was an absolutely perfect night had Matipa not shown up halfway through dinner, decked out in a figure-hugging, shimmering red organza dress with a long tail. The dress had an incredibly low back. No, that is actually an understatement, there was no back. Her braided her had been coiled into a bun on top of her head. I hate to say this but she looked amazing. I understood then the attraction between her and my husband. I could tell the guests were a little confused by her presence. Here we were, celebrating our seventeenth anniversary and Jonasi's mistress shows up. My mother threw me a knowing look. A look that communicated a thousand words. I wanted to dig a hole and die. I don't think there's a greater humiliation than that. Before I had walked around confidently, strutting like a peacock, but after Matipa arrived I wanted the earth to open up and swallow me. However I felt my anxiety melt as Jonasi put a reassuring arm around me. That gesture alone seemed to restore my confidence. This was my night; I would be damned if Matipa would ruin it for me. After dinner, Jonasi and I stood up to cut the cake just as we had at our wedding. He fed it to me then kissed the cream off my lips. Then he really kissed me. There was deafening applause all around me. After that I tell you the party carried on in a blur of happy faces. I drank champagne and danced with my husband, my children, my guests and my husband again. All I know is that I tumbled into bed at 2 a.m. and Jonasi was beside me, trying to get me out of my suit as fast as he could. I'll stop here because big girls don't kiss and tell. But I'll tell you something... it was a amazing night, I mean morning!

seven

They say big girls don't cry but I promise you I howled the night of that anniversary party. I think I must have cried so hard I woke up the neighbours. I'm known for a lot of things but being a cry-baby isn't one of them. I usually make other people cry. I fired my last PA because she was too emotional calling me a slave-driver! So there I was, the tough cookie being reduced to a pool of tears. You see I left the party just before midnight like Cinderella. It was not my intention to leave so early. My intention had been to leave with Jonasi but I left the party running for life after this mad-looking matronly woman threatened to maul me in the bathroom. You know what they say, once beaten, twice shy. When I got home I took a bath and sat in my satin robe on the balcony listening to the birds chirping. It was a beautiful night actually, with a clear cloudless sky. The weather was perfect for an outdoor party. I lit a cigarette. (Something I do when I'm stressed. Jonasi doesn't even know I smoke. It's a bad habit I picked up at university). I smoked and drank red wine and waited for Jonasi to come home. You see I was pissed off; extremely pissed off. I would look at my watch and I tell you the smoke coming out of my ears was not from the cigarettes. I called Jonasi a couple of times and he was not answering his phone. At first I thought he might not be able to hear the phone ring above the loud noise of the party. But when I called him again at 4 a.m. and his phone was switched off I threw my diamante-studded Samsung against the wall. Jonasi would have to make sure he replaced it. I opened another bottle of wine and drank until the sun came up. I was bawling my eyes out by then. I cursed Joyce and her fucking party. You see, three weeks ago we got these invitation cards from Joyce. I tell you Jonasi was fuming. In all the time I had known him he rarely lost his cool but that day it was like he was on fire. He was adamant that he was not going and that he was going to fix Joyce. Then a week ago these expensive suits were delivered to the office and I was like, "So what's the occasion?"

"I have to go to this thing. Joyce's father threatened to get my banking licence revoked if I don't go."

"I don't believe this!" I cried out.

"Trust me, I do."

"I'm coming with you," I declared.

"Trust me you don't want to do that. Let me handle this on my own. Her father will be there. I don't want to ruffle his feathers. It could be bad for my business. "

"Jonasi this isn't fair! Joyce has you by the balls!"

He smiled wryly, "Yes she does, doesn't she?"

Still I was pissed off about the whole thing, especially when Jonasi left work after lunch to prepare. He said he needed to get a haircut and a shave. That was bullshit. Worse still everybody in the office was talking about the anniversary party and talking about me. You know that feeling when you just know the minute you turn your back little motormouths are running. I decided then I was going to the party and left the office to look for a dress. I headed off to Sam Levy's and combed the boutiques for something glamorous to wear. I had every right to be at that party, after all Joyce had extended an invite to me as well. It was a wonderful event. I have to give credit where it's due. The food was great, so was the décor. But I did feel a little out of place. No actually I felt largely out of place. Most of the guests were couples and there I was, looking lonesome and sticking out like a sore thumb. Yes it was my intention to make a grand entrance but I was so embarrassed when they could not find a place to seat me.

"I have a card," I said trying to keep my voice down.

I was ready to cause a scene if need be.

The party hostess was apologetic, "I'm sure there was a small mistake. Not to worry, I'll seat you."

I was seated at some table at the back of the garden with a bunch of nobodies. Not one person who I could recognise from anywhere. They were a talkative bunch and the women could not help oohing and aaahing over Mr and Mrs Gomora. You should have heard the comments:

"They are such a beautiful couple...."

"They have such beautiful children...."

"And they have such a beautiful house!"

"And they are so in love after all these years. Some people are blessed...."

I almost choked on my drink. I was tempted to tell them that the illusion of the fairy-tale life the Gomoras gave did not have the proverbial happy-ever-after ending. That Jonasi had been living with me for over a year now. They could take their happily-ever-after bullshit and shove it up their asses! To add insult to injury, Jonasi acknowledged my presence with a skirting "hello". Look,

I was not expecting him to grab the mic and introduce me to everyone but such an impersonal greeting to someone he shared a home with? Hello! He acted like we were business partners or something. I think we spoke for like a minute and even then his eyes were already searching the crowd for Joyce. I know he was putting up a show for his father-in-law but somehow I was not convinced he was still acting out a charade. He looked like he was enjoying it. So I sat in the wings and drank, waiting for the curtain to come down. A politician came up and started chatting me up. I engaged him, batting my eyelids coyly. That would teach Jonasi a lesson. However my little game was cut short by that bitch who accosted me in the bathroom...

I spent my Sunday vacillating between crying and sleeping and hoping that Jonasi would come home. He did not. Monday I called in sick at work and spent the day hoping he would come round. Surely he would care if I did not show up at work? The day ended wordlessly. No phone calls, no text message, no nothing! I tried to call him but his phone was switched off. I tried his other cell phone and it was also switched off. When I woke up on Tuesday and looked at myself in the mirror I shuddered. I looked like shit. I told myself then that this nonsense had to stop. I had to pull myself together and fast. I booked myself into Clinique for a manicure and a pedicure, had a facial done and a full body massage. I spent the rest of the afternoon shopping and got a little replacement phone until Jonasi decided to get me a better one. That evening I did get a call, but it was not from Jonasi, it was from Comrade Zhou, the politician from the party. He said I never said "goodbye" and I told him I had the runs. He said had been trying to call me all weekend. I lied and said my phone was bust and he promised to get me another one. I did not say "no" but I did not say "yes" either. He invited me out for dinner. Turns out he was actually the ambassador to China. He worked in Beijing but lived in Guangzhou wherever that was. He said he was flying out the next day and suggested I visit.

"What about your wife and three kids?" I asked coyly

"Something can be sorted out," he said matter-of-factly.

"I'll think about it," I replied.

When I went to the bathroom to touch up my make-up it hit me that life after Jonasi would not be rosy. Where would I get another technocrat to top Jonasi's looks and wealth? I promise you if Jonasi left me I had to make sure the next man I got into a relationship with had more money and more power than Jonasi. But where in Zimbabwe was I going to get a man who could outrank Jonasi unless I dated the president himself? At this rate I would be forced to spread my wings into SADC and suss out any eligible presidents there. To be honest with you; I'm not a political aficionado. The thought of wearing a *doekie* and singing at political rallies did not excite me one bit. But that could easily change if there was a vacancy for First Lady. I would be the one in the front line donned in army print cargo pants wearing a tight vest with the President's face on screaming at the top of the lungs. There is no bigger motivator than money and power. I exhaled deeply. I had to think, and I had to think strategically. I went back to the table and finished off my dessert with Mr Guangzhou. We parted with a polite peck on the cheek. I was not ready to compromise myself or my relationship with Jonasi just yet.

The next day I decided to go into work. I was dressed to the nines and looked like a million dollars. Ladies you must always look the part. You dress like 10 cents and you'll be treated like you are worth 10 cents. I made a detour past Jonasi's office only to have his PA tell me that Jonasi had taken two weeks off from work.

"I thought you knew," she said, avoiding looking at me in the eye.

"Was it this week?" I replied nonchalantly, trying to mask my surprise.

"Yes it is," she replied. "He took Joyce on a seven-day cruise in the Mediterranean. The children will join them in Italy for another week. Isn't that a nice anniversary present? Some women have..."

I knew the last bit of information was offered with obvious malice. Jonasi's PA had never liked me. I figured at some point Jonasi must have screwed her otherwise where would the beef be coming from?

"Don't you have any work to do?" I asked, cutting her off abruptly, "I know Jonasi doesn't pay you to gossip."

I turned and walked off to my office and collapsed in my chair. I sat there staring at my computer screen, unable to work. Just for a split second I contemplated throwing myself off the tenth floor. I would be dead by the time I hit the ground. I imagined my bloodied body splattered all over Union Avenue. Jonasi would be consumed by guilt. For the rest of his fucking life he would have my blood on his hands. However I knew there was no way I could kill myself. I was too strong for that kind of bullshit. Instead I picked up the phone and called Mr. Guangzhou. I told him I was going to take him up on the China trip. A holiday did no one any harm. After all Jonasi was sunning his black ass out in the Mediterranean. After I hung up I went to Jonasi's PA to tell her I would be away for three weeks and that if anyone needed me I would be unreachable.

eight

When I saw Jonasi's Mercedes pull up outside my house I knew there was trouble in paradise. He'd never drive out all this way usually. We had not seen Jonasi in this neck of the woods for ages. I poured myself a stiff glass of whisky because I knew I was going to need it. Nowadays I had to be mellow to deal with Jonasi. If I was too sober I was afraid I would beat him to death. From my kitchen window I could see him park his car out in the street. That was a sure sign he was not staying long. I can't even remember the last time Jonasi slept at my place. Worse still I can't even remember the last time I had sex with Jonasi. It must have been back in the nineties. Not that I miss it. I have had enough sex to last me a lifetime. The dirty children that had been playing on the street stood there in awe of him. It's not every day that they see a clean-shaven, well-presented man in a million-dollar pinstriped suit who drove a million-dollar car. The men in their lives were dirty, smelly drunkards, some who stole for a living. The township had few role models for these young impressionable children. Even without seeing them, I knew my neighbours were hanging out of their windows to get a glimpse of Jonasi. You see when you live in the location everyone wants to know your business. You can't fart without anyone knowing about it. But this is where I grew up and this is where I want to die. I could have lived up in the uppity suburbs of Harare if I had wanted to but hell no; no one knows me there. What's the point of success if those who saw you grow up struggling can't see it? I want to be seen. And trust me; they see me in my red BMW. They see me when I wake up in the morning and stand out on my balcony overlooking the tiny matchbox houses in the township. And I am proud to say I am the only one who lives in a double-storey home on my street. People have tried to emulate me, but most of the houses here are standing with no roofs. I am the trendsetter here. Everyone wants to be like me. Everything always looks rosy from the outside.

"Jonasi, darling!" I gushed as I opened my arms to him.

I enveloped him in my bosom. My breasts were like pillows and Jonasi loved to rest his head on them. He was lost in their warmth. I could feel the tension in him slowly dissipate. I knew Jonasi too well. I could read him like a fortune teller.

"Essie, it's been long," he sighed, "Too long."

"It has. I've missed you too!"

I had surpassed the stage of missing Jonasi. But I guess that's what he wanted to hear. So I told him that to make him happy. Men are all the same. They just want their egos pampered and Jonasi is no different. He entered my house and collapsed onto the leather Lazy Boy. I put his feet up on a foot stool and removed his socks and shoes. Then I poured him a glass of Glenfiddich Whiskey. I always kept some in anticipation of his visits. I had to hide it from my first-born son, Freedom, a bona fide alcoholic.

"Can I bring you some food?" I asked.

"Please. I haven't had anything to eat since this morning."

I wobbled off to the kitchen, my buttocks shaking from side to side. I am not a small woman. Even when I was young I had extremely large buttocks and extremely huge breasts and this tiny little waist. My disproportionate body used to bother me until I realised it is what brought the boys to the yard. I heated up some leftover tripe-and-onion stew. Then I made him a pot of piping hot *sadza*. Jonasi loved his *sadza*. I suspected Joyce never cooked it for him. She did not look like the type to cook *sadza*, probably had Jonasi on a staple of rice and macaroni. If I could have a chance to sit down with her I could probably tell her a thing or two about Jonasi. I've known Jonasi for a long time. We literally grew up in the same neighbourhood, playing together in the dust and dirt of Highfields. Jonasi's mother died when he was just three. He was the youngest in a family of four boys. After his mother died, a lot of women used to drift in and out of their lives, however none stayed for the long haul. Jonasi's dad worked at Natbrew Breweries and drank as a hobby. His parenting skills were non-existent so little Jonasi practically lived in our house. He used to sleep on the floor next to me, my breasts a cushion for his head. I suppose he felt neglected. His father did not have time for him. His older brothers ignored him and kicked him about when they felt like it. I took him under my wing. He was four years younger than me. I loved him like the little brother I never had. I had no idea Jonasi's love for me went beyond the brotherly and sisterly kind until one day when we were in high school. I was walking home from school with this guy that I liked. He innocently put his arms around me and hugged me. Jonasi saw us and beat the poor guy to a pulp, never mind that he was older and in the sixth form. I guess growing up in the streets with four bullying brothers had toughened Jonasi in a big way.

"I'm going to marry you Essie," he said. "Don't waste your time with these stupid township boys. I will work hard and get us out of this mess."

I laughed in derision. I did not believe him. I saw him as another dreamer like all the township boys around me. I wanted to use my pretty face to get out of the location. I never did. I ended up pregnant at sixteen by some good-for-nothing soldier. As soon as my tummy was bulging for everyone to see, Jonasi stopped talking to me. In his letters, the soldier promised to marry me but was killed in the bush and never lived to see the Independence he fought for. I gave birth to a bouncing baby boy that I named Freedom. Jonasi hated that child. He still does. I never went back to school. I worked here and there just to support my child. I even started going out with this businessman who used to give me money. When Jonasi found out he beat me till I had nearly lost all consciousness. Then he raped me, repeatedly.

"I'm your man, don't you ever forget that."

That was how my second child was conceived. Jonasi named her Sarah after his late mother. He was at varsity then but somehow he wangled money here and there to support us but it was never easy. I still lived at home and now I had two kids and my mother would complain that I was not pulling my weight. She despised Jonasi even more and would tell me repeatedly that he would never do anything for me. At times I would sleep with other men just to make ends meet. One day Jonasi caught me having sex in the back seat of a man's car. He beat me up so bad I had to be hospitalised. He would call me a whore and every other name under the sun but when the dust settled we would be alright again. My mother told me over and over again that nothing would come from our relationship. She was right because Jonasi went and married Joyce and they had a big fancy wedding. I knew why he had not married me; I was not the loyal, unwavering partner that he wanted. That had been Joyce's forte. She had believed in him, believed in him with all her heart. All I had to ride on was that I was the first woman Jonasi loved and I knew deep down he would always love me. My mother thought I was delusional but Jonasi came through for me. He took care of me like he said he would. In 1991 he came to my parents and said he wanted to take me as his second wife. They agreed and he paid the lobola. Our second child, Blessing, was born a year after. Not too long after that I was diagnosed with cervical cancer and had my uterus removed in the process. What did I want more children for? Joyce was doing a pretty good job of carrying on the family name. Last I heard she was on child number five.

I served Jonasi the food and he ate like a ravenous street kid. Afterwards he relaxed on the couch, his head on my lap. He fell asleep there. In the old days I would enjoy watching him sleep. Now I could not wait to throw him off my lap and get on with the dishes. But just as well I did this once in a while. I felt sorry for whoever had to put up with Jonasi on a daily basis. He was physically and emotionally draining and basically everything revolved around him. It was all about him, the selfish prick. I reached for his glass of whiskey and emptied it.

"You know I feel so at ease when I'm here with you,"

he said when he woke up.

I stroked his head affectionately and did not say anything.

"You know, Essie, I'm so stressed."

"What is it? Work?"

"Work is fine. The business is doing great. I can't believe how well we are doing."

If it was not work then it had something to do with a woman. Look, I have been around a long time. I had seen girls drift in and out of Jonasi's life. When I was younger, I would be consumed with jealousy but as I got older I had started to care less. It was always the same, when things were going well with the new woman you would not see Jonasi for dust. However let the relationship hit a snag and he would be at my doorstep crying like a wounded dog. It's true, every dog finds its way home, whether it's to Folyjon Crescent or Warren Park D.

"What is it then? Joycie and the kids bothering you?" I asked, trying to act concerned.

He exhaled deeply, "Joyce and the kids are fine. We went on holiday together. First I took Joyce on this cruise. You know we haven't been alone since Shumi was born and it was good to get away. We really had a great time. We connected again."

He seemed reflective, far away, and then as an afterthought quickly added, "I should also take you there some time."

He wouldn't. Jonasi had never taken me anywhere outside this township. I guess I could have taken myself somewhere but I was not interested in that kind of thing. I just want money. Hard cash that I can touch and feel. I can proudly say that Jonasi has made sure that I am well taken care of. My car is fully paid off and I get a salary like every other employee on his payroll, except

I don't work for it. (Trust me I paid my dues a long time ago.) In the past, I was a bona fide shopaholic. I would shop until my joints ached. I was on a first-name basis with most of the boutique owners and department store managers in Harare. Whenever they had new stock I would get a call. I had ladies who brought Dubai, London and Johannesburg to my doorstep. I was the best-dressed lady in the township but now the only place I get dressed for is church. My priorities have changed considerably. You see I sinned a long time ago and now I am praying for redemption. The only shopping I do now is for my children. They are my biggest concern now. Blessing is only eleven and still has a long way to get through school. Sarah will be starting varsity soon. As long as Jonasi breathes I know he will take care of them but the day he drops dead all hell will break loose. I have no idea how much that pie of his will have to be split. I know about Joyce and her troop but I cannot say with certainty that there are no other little satellite families like mine out there.

"There's this girl. Matipa. We really understand each other."

So this was the mystery lady who had been keeping his engine oiled lately.

"She's brilliant. She's intelligent. We are on the same wavelength. We can talk about stuff. I feel like I've met my match with her. You know she energises me...."

You see this is what I mean when I say Jonasi is a selfish bastard. He expects you to sit and listen about his latest whore and not bat an eyelid. How many times did he slap me for batting my eyelids at other men?

"So what's the problem then?" I asked, hoping he would wrap it up soon.

"She's young. She wants to get married. I want to marry her."

"So marry her Jonasi. Why don't you marry her?"

"I'm not sure if Joyce will agree and I'm not sure if she'll want to be number three."

Not many people know about me. Even Joyce doesn't know about me. I'm the fat second wife who lives in obscurity in the location away from the high life.

"You'll make a plan Jonasi, you always do," I replied dismissively and stood up to start on the dishes.

"Essie come back here," he said, "We haven't finished."

We had. We had been finished a long time ago. However I did not have the balls to tell him that so instead I returned to his side and let him tell me about the new love of his life.

nine

The flight back from China was long and uneventful. I had plenty of time to think. Time to evaluate my options, if you could even call them that. My illicit rendezvous with Mr Guangzhou had done a lot to recharge my batteries. It's amazing how a change of dick can put things into a clearer perspective. His shagging had really taken the edge off me. I was starting to get paranoid about Jonasi. Actually I was becoming too attached to Jonasi for my own good. And he had showed me that night that our attachment could be fleeting. Well fuck him, two can play that game and after China I was ready to face the world. Mr Guangzhou had really treated me well. He had put me up in this nice five-star hotel with room service and the works. Of course he could not spend time with me willy-nilly because his wife had his balls in her Gucci handbag. It made me realise just how fortunate I was to have free rein over Jonasi. I mean I literally lived with the man. Another thing I took for granted was money. Jonasi gave me real money. Not plastic money like Mr Guangzhou. I managed to max out his credit cards but left China without a dime. If I needed money I would have to sell the gold chains around my neck and the bangles on my wrists. Customs would probably harass me because I looked like a mobile jewellery shop. I had gold in my ears, gold on my fingers and gold on my toes. What was left for me was to have gold hanging out of my anus. What I knew for sure is that I had a gold mine back home. Jonasi had brought me my own penthouse. The Ballantyne Park home would only ever be signed over to me if I popped a child of his. So in a lot of respects I had to count my blessings. Not to forget we had great sex. Some men just don't get you there. They take you by the hand and leave you halfway. But Jonasi rides me to kingdom come and all the way back. So when I weighed the pros and cons of being in a relationship with Jonasi versus being alone, the scale was weighted in his favour. Look I'd had a good dose of realism these past three weeks. The sad reality is Joyce is not going anywhere. If you were in her shoes you'd also not be going anywhere in a rush. So it's either I sit it out or wait for her to drop dead. Trust me that thought of an expired Joyce has crossed my mind a thousand times. I often wished Joyce would have a heart attack or drive over a cliff but those kinds of things only happen in movies. Joyce is here to stay. It's pitiful really. Joyce has no leg to stand on without Jonasi. What's left is for Jonasi to breathe air into her lungs. Without Jonasi she would be like a deflated balloon. So what option do I have but to coexist with her? I know you are probably thinking I'm settling for second best but I am not. What other options do I have? That's not really true. I have lots of options as my mother always tells me. She says I should just find a decent young man and settle down. What she really means is that I should just find a poor bastard and we scratch a living together. She always goes on about how many men are out there with potential, that these very men will become the next Jonasi, given a chance. I don't know if I have the patience to sit around waiting for someone's potential to materialise. What if it never does? Then I'd be stuck with a poor bastard who never realised his full potential. I mean why not just get someone who has already reached his full potential then you don't have to gamble on the unknown? My older sister married someone who supposedly had potential. They have been married for ten years and the only potential he realised was becoming an unemployed overweight bully who beats up my sister when the urge takes him. My sister has to support him and his whole family. They move around in the same tired car they had ten years ago and make no mistake about it, my sister is not happy. Look I can't say I am one hundred-percent happy with the status quo with Jonasi. However I am happy most of the time. I have a lot more than most people can hope for in a lifetime and for now it will have to do.

So I eventually fell asleep knowing what my next move on the chess board would be. When I woke up I was back in Harare. I had arranged for the driver to pick me up. To my surprise he drove me to the penthouse.

"Is there anything we need here?" I asked from behind my Prada sunglasses.

"The boss had all your belongings moved back to Northfields."

I could have pissed on myself right then. What the hell was going on? I had been away for three weeks and already I had been displaced.

"Okay then," I replied with insouciance.

No need to give away anything to the driver.

I swung out of the car and made my way back up to the tenth floor. I won't lie; it was good to be back. I sat on the balcony smoking and tried to call Jonasi. He was unreachable. Out of desperation I called the landline at Joyce's home. The maid said they had gone out; the whole family had gone out to dinner. I swore again and decided I needed a stiff drink and tried not to feel like a discarded condom.

Even when I went to work the next day I was not sure what to expect. I almost thought the guards would grab me and tell me that I was barred from entering the building. Nothing of the sort happened. I made my way into my office and my PA was quick to update me on what had been happening. On the top of the list was that Jonasi wanted to meet with me urgently. I wondered what for, to get me to sign my severance package? She slated a meeting for 10 o'clock. I tell you I was wrought with anxiety by the time I marched into his office, but I reached into my inner reserves for an injection of bravado.

"Matipa, where the hell have you been?" he shouted.

"Good morning to you, Jonasi," I replied, "I missed you Jonasi. Did you miss me?"

I really had missed him. Seeing him sent shockwaves through my whole body. Gosh I could not believe it had been this long.

"Matipa, cut the bullshit, where have you been?"

"Where have I been? Where have you been? You go on some cruise without telling me –"

"Shut up," he roared, "This is not about me it's about you. I was with my wife and kids. You knew I had a wife and four kids when you met me!"

Now that statement irritated the shit out of me. You have no idea just how much. How dare he throw that "wife and four kids" story back at me? How dare he?

"The last time I checked, Jonasi, I didn't have a husband that I answer to," I replied coolly.

Jonasi's eyes were burning like coal. "Matipa where were you?" he asked me through gritted teeth.

"Jonasi," I replied calmly, "I went to China with my mother. Not that it's any of your business."

He grabbed me by the neck and I thought he would strangle the life out of me. I had never seen him so incensed, so outraged.

"Matipa, don't lie to me!"

"Jonasi," I choked, "You're hurting me."

I felt his grip loosen around me. I massaged my neck, trying to obliterate the pain he had caused me in a few seconds.

"Don't ever touch me like that again," I hissed.

"I'm sorry," he apologised.

I was not moved.

"I know it hasn't occurred to you but I do have a mother and father who are appalled that I live with a married man. My parents can't even visit me because of you. I have sacrificed a lot to be with you and for what? So that you can stand there like a sanctimonious jerk and give me the third degree? I don't need this kind of bullshit Jonasi. You can take your wife and four kids and shove them up your ass!"

"Matipa I was worried. You disappear for three weeks and don't say anything!"

"But it's okay for you to disappear with your wife and four kids? What did you expect me to do?"

"Look I'm sorry, but I explained the situation to you. I can't afford to upset Joyce at the moment."

"But you can afford to upset me?"

"Look I'll make it up to you Matipa. I'll take you anywhere you want."

"Jonasi you can take me to the moon and back but it won't cut it. I want to get married. That's what I want. I want you to be able to sit down at the same table with my parents. Right now I'm nothing more than a glorified mistress. You think I like the way I was treated at the party?"

"Matipa I explained to you why I had to do that. I can't afford to mess around with Joyce's dad. We'll both end up on the streets."

"Okay fine then. Take me as your second wife. Joyce can stay but make me your second wife."

"Okay fine."

I was not appeased. That sounded too easy, much too easy. I was not going to be fooled with sweet nothings. I wanted concrete promises.

"I want a date Jonasi. I want a written and signed affidavit that you will marry me."

He laughed then. The tension had dissolved from his brow.

"We'll do it this weekend. I will meet with your aunt and we'll set things up for this weekend."

And just like that I negotiated my way into Jonasi's harem.

Jonasi, in the company of his older brothers, Wonder and Gershom came to negotiate the lobola. Jonasi's father was late and so Wonder had assumed the role of being head of the family. His brothers were nothing like him. They were older, weather-beaten men who I doubt had ever seen better days. Jonasi had told me that there was another brother who had been killed in a brawl in a beer hall. Wonder ran a bottle store and butchery in Budiriro and Gershom had a fleet of minibus taxis. Jonasi had explained to me that he had set them up because he was tired of them begging for money from him. He confessed that he had to bail them out of financial fixes every now and then. They smelled of trouble and looked like they would steal from Jonasi if they were given the remotest chance. They were the kind of men you wanted to watch your back around. But I smiled at them anyway then because they had come to further my ambition of being married to Jonasi. Being polite and cordial to them for a few hours would not break my back but God help me if I ever had to entertain those bastards again. My father welcomed Jonasi's entourage with open arms. I have not told you yet about my father. He's the male version of a gold digger. He would have married me off to anything just as long as it had money. Now you see where I got it from. My mother was the only one who was outraged by the whole scenario. She thought I was crazy to willingly enter into a polygamous marriage. She was still angry with my father for going along with the whole charade but he had dismissed her with a slap across her face. She had tried to plead with me the night before not to go through it.

"Why settle for being second best in a man's life?"

I looked at her with pity in my eyes, "You are Dad's first wife and he treats you like a fucking second-class citizen."

That silenced my mother. We had watched how our father had abused her throughout their marriage and she did not even have the guts to stand up to him. Now she wanted to preach to me about being second best.

"And for the record mama, I'm not second best," I responded acidly. "It's not my fault Joyce was born earlier."

She was there by default. Got knocked up and Jonasi had to marry her. I was there because he wanted me to be there.

"Do you think what you are doing is right?"

"Yes Mum. It has never felt so right," I replied indignantly.

"You reap what you sow," replied my mother.

I had reaped for sure. Jonasi was charged ten cows plus a fat load of cash. With that ceremony concluded I was now legit. My father threw a huge party at home for all our close family and friends. I know I had to give up my grand wedding plans but it seemed a small sacrifice in the grand scheme of things. Jonasi gave me the Ballantyne Park house as a wedding present. He also bought me a huge diamond ring. I was now fully armed to step into the future with a little more confidence about my position in Jonasi's life. Now I was Jonasi's wife.

ten

I am happy to say that our marriage survived the Matipa debacle. Jonasi and I got through it and emerged stronger than ever. You see after our anniversary party Jonasi moved back home. He ended the affair with Matipa. He also assured me that Matipa was relieved of her duties at J&J Holdings. I forgave Jonasi for his infidelity and we moved on from it. Matipa was a thing of the past. I would be lying if I said things were the same; they were not. They were ten times better. Jonasi was really trying to make things work. He was loving, attentive and everything else I wanted him to be. At first I was filled with mistrust but he assured me he did not want to jeopardise our family life again and I believed him. He still worked odd hours and travelled abroad on business but he came home to us and over time my fears of him leaving me were put to rest. The sex was explosive and he even joked that we should have another child. My mother said she would box me if I had another child with Jonasi. I was not sure about having another baby. Look I was 36 then; did I really want to be changing diapers well into my forties? My body was back in the shape I wanted it to be in. I had never looked better. I wanted to face my forties looking fabulous, not with a folded tummy and fleshy thighs. However Jonasi was really putting on the pressure. Shumi had just started Grade 1 and he insisted there was no better time to have another child. He said he wanted a girl this time around. Rudo was all grown up and was no longer his little girl. She was now a temperamental teenager who could not wait to see the back of her father.

"You'd be a fool to have another baby," my mother remarked. "Besides, there are probably bigger fools out there having his babies."

"Mum please. Don't start on that."

"Look what happened with your father," she replied.

My father had died two years before from leukaemia. At the funeral, full-grown men and women came crawling out of the earth claiming to be his children from another mother. My mother had chased them away.

"You can be his children in the next life. In this life he only had three kids. If you think you'll get a cent, think again. Just get the hell off my property before I shoot you all."

They had tried to get loud and dangerous about the house we had grown up in. The cars my father drove. Even the clothes he wore. My mother had thrown them in a heap in the driveway and had watched with humour as they grappled for his old shirts and trousers. My father had left no will and there was only $50 left in his entire estate. That managed to quiet all the wannabe children.

"Mum," I said, "Move in with us. I'll take care of you," I volunteered.

I was outraged that my father had left nothing for her.

My sisters and I were married and had our husbands to look after us but what about Mum?

"I am happy here," she would say, "This is where I'm closest to your father."

"But Mum he left nothing!" I protested, "What will you survive on?"

"That's the nice thing about losing your spouse to a chronic illness," said my mother with a toothy grin, "You have time to prepare."

Before my father died she said she had transferred all the assets he had into her name and had left only $50 in his bank account. There was no will to contest or anything.

"Joyce, if you want my advice you will start doing the same. The way your husband enjoys spreading love around like he's spreading the gospel! You and your four kids will be fighting for the crumbs with the rest of Africa I tell you."

"Mum he's changed."

"Huh," she snorted, "A leopard never changes its spots. The best thing you can do for yourself is get your tubes tied and start doing something constructive with your life. If there was a Nobel Prize for having babies you would have won it. Four times!"

To put the baby story to rest I decided to follow her advice. I also decided not to tell Jonasi about my decision because I knew he would not agree to it. So I conveniently picked a time when he was away on business to check into hospital. The doctor assured me it was a quick procedure and I would be hospitalised overnight. My mother said she would hold the fort at home until I got out. I was actually very nervous. I hated keeping secrets from Jonasi. Wasn't that what marriage was about, sharing everything? Of course my mother thought I was delusional.

"You think Jonasi tells you everything?"

"Yes," I replied.

She snorted with derision, "You don't know the half of it. Men are sneaky creatures. Look at your father."

You see now that just pisses me off. I hate my mother at times for being the thorn in my side. She's negative about everything. She could be annoying at times, especially since I could see how hard Jonasi was trying. We were happy, really happy. Things were good. Jonasi's relationship with the kids had improved dramatically and he was more involved with them and related to them like human beings. The business was doing extremely well. J&J Holdings was now listed on the London Stock Exchange. I now shopped in Oxford Street in London and 5th Avenue in New York. Tino had started university at the London Business School where he was going to major in economics. Jonasi was grooming him to take over the family business. Rudo was now sitting her 'O' Levels. Gari would be starting high school soon. Every night I thanked God for his blessings. Things could not have been any better.

"So who is your husband screwing now?" continued my mother.

She's so relentless. She just doesn't know when to give up. Sometimes I think she does not want to see me happy. Why can't she let Jonasi be just for a minute?

"Mum let it go. We are happy. We have never been happier."

She rolled her eyes heavenward like I was talking bullshit. That irked me even more. Sometimes I wonder why I even listen to her. I was glad when the nurses came to prepare me for the operation. She wanted to stay but I told her to go. I'd had enough of her for one day. She kissed me goodbye and said she would see me the next morning.

But you know what, when I woke up from the operation in excruciating pain she was there to hold my hand and annoy the shit out of me. She finally left at midnight after the nurses told her I really had to get some rest. You see even the nurses were scared of her.

When I woke up the next morning I called my sister Jennifer. Not the one married to the white American. Jennifer, my other sister who lives in South Africa with her high flying husband, a marketing executive. Jennifer is an engineer. I guess I am the underachiever in our family. So anyway, I called Jenny to tell her I was in hospital, getting my tubes tied. I told her I was quite sad about it.

"Why?" she said. "You already have four."

You see Jenny only has one child and has never wanted to have more.

"That's the same thing Mum said."

"For once I agree with Mum," she replied.

Neither of my sisters gets along with my mother. They say she's a controlling voracious bully. Being the youngest, I guess I got caught up in her web.

"She says I shouldn't tell Jonasi. I just don't think its right that I keep secrets from him."

"Look sweetie, you should tell him if you want to. It's your marriage. Don't let Mum control you too much okay? I have to go. I have a meeting at nine. Get well soon and tell mum to eff off if she bothers you."

She hung up then and I lay in bed staring at the ceiling. I was bored and had no idea when they intended to discharge me. I yearned for the comfort of my home. I wanted to get back into the activities of dropping off and picking up my children from school. Supervising their homework and making packed lunches. Mundane things that I took great pleasure in; things that would undoubtedly drive my mother crazy. Just as well Rudo was a weekly border so I did not have to worry about her. I scrolled through my phone thinking maybe I should call Jonasi but he was in Washington and he was probably not awake yet. The nurse brought me breakfast and some painkillers. I ate out of boredom more than anything. Hospital food was shit; it made me miss home even more. I had just finished taking my medication when the doctor arrived.

"How is Mrs Gomora doing?" he asked.

Gawd, I had not been called that in a very long time. It sounded alien to my ears.

"I'm doing okay," I replied, giving him a winning smile like I was in a Colgate advert.

The truth was that I ached like a motherfucker, but I just wanted to go home and lie in my own bed. He did the usual tests: temperature, blood pressure, heart, lungs and then felt my tummy a bit. Though I had to wonder about the necessity of that.

"You are recovering well Mrs Gomora," he said, "I'll discharge you today."

"I can't wait."

"You Gomora women are tough. I have another patient, Matipa Gomora, are you related?"

"Matipa who?" I almost choked.

"Matipa Gomora. She's in maternity though. Tough cookie that one."

I felt the bacon bits and scrambled eggs begin to churn inside my stomach.

"Matipa who?"

"Matipa Chando Gomora," he repeated.

There was only one Matipa I knew and as far as I believed she wasn't a Gomora. My husband had brothers but none of their wives answered to that name. Besides, the last I heard they could not afford to give birth in private hospitals.

"I suppose you don't know her," he said dismissively. "It's just that Gomora is not a common name."

"No it's not," I replied, trying to gain some measure of self-control.

"Anyway I'm going to sign you out. Get dressed and go home."

I could not move. My legs were numb and heavy as lead. I tried to muster the strength to move but I felt like I was stapled to the bed. My mother arrived, wearing one of her signature caftans. She looked frightened and frantic. One look at her and my stomach did somersaults. The room started to spin and I felt like I was caught up in a whirlwind.

"Joyce did you call Jonasi?"she hissed, trying to keep her voice down. "I bumped into him in the corridor."

My throat was dry. I could not speak and just shook my head.

"Well his car is outside. I thought you said he was in Washington? I had to use the steps. Ten thousand fucking steps. You have no idea how tired I am...."

I don't know what she said afterwards. I collapsed then and as my mother later narrated, fell off the bed.

eleven

Motherhood is truly a miracle. I could not believe I had given birth to a set of beautiful twin girls. They were really gorgeous. I could not stop staring at them. There is something magical about bringing life into the world. To think that my lovemaking with Jonasi had created these two little angels was truly overwhelming. They had a bit of us in them. I can't really explain it. I felt such incredulous love for them. I don't even know if that is the right word. I felt something towards them that I had never felt before. Not even for Jonasi. My darling husband was equally enamoured with his girls. I was actually surprised. You would think after having so many kids he wouldn't care less about mine but he adored the twins. I guess they were a novelty. (Joyce had not produced twins so I was one up on her in that regard.) If I had known having his children would have evoked such a reaction out of him I would have had them a long time ago. While I was convalescing at home after being discharged from hospital he gave me the keys to a brand new Cherokee Jeep fitted with identical baby seats. You're damn right

I was happy. Whilst he was still riding on the crest of joy I insisted that he establish a trust fund for the girls where he would deposit wads of money every month. I might have been bleeding buckets but I got out of bed to discuss setting the fund up with his lawyers in New York. I would be the sole administrator until the girls reached 21. Not only did I have to take care of number one, I now had my girls to take care of. And where better to have offshore funds than where I knew no one would touch them, especially Joyce?

The reality was I was illegal and she was legal. Yes I used Mrs Gomora when it suited me but in all honesty I had no rights to that name. My girls did though and I was going to make sure that they had rights to the Gomora money too. We need to stop calling them my girls. They have names after all: Ashley and Hayley. Even before they were born those are the names I wanted for them. Of course Jonasi wanted to saddle them with some crazy Shona names so they ended up being Ashley Panashe and Hayley Munashe Gomora. You have no idea how I hated those names. Every other Shona child is called Panashe, Munashe, Tinashe, Ruvarashe....it sounds like a fucking nursery rhyme. So now my kids sound like every other kid on the block. But what to do? It's what their father wanted and what Jonasi wanted, Jonasi got, inevitably. We were one big happy family now. I had done my part for motherhood, carried the banner high, but trust me I was not going to have any more children. As soon as it was possible I was also going to have my tubes tied. I think between Joyce and me there are enough of Jonasi's children to carry the family name. I'm sure you know now that Joyce knows about Ashley and Hayley. It's actually very funny how she found out. Okay it was not really funny, more like shock horror. Well it turns out we were in the same hospital at the same time. How ironic is that? She was there to get her tubes tied and I was there to give birth. Jonasi knew when I would be going in to give birth so he just told Joyce he would be overseas for two weeks. It was the perfect plan. He did that all the time if he wanted to spend quality time with me. Joyce would never suspect a thing. Sometimes he would genuinely go overseas and I would accompany him. However towards the end of my pregnancy I was in no position to fly so he would take Joyce. We had some kind of roster going. Except that Joyce did not know about it. But I was happy now that she knew about everything.

She came to my private ward to visit. We were not expecting her. There was Jonasi doing the balancing act with the twins in his arms and Joyce walked in. Not far behind was that woman I had a nasty encounter with in the bathroom at their seventeenth anniversary party. The nameless woman who I soon learned was Joyce's mother. Jonasi saved the day and managed to get things under control. He took Joyce home but her mother stayed behind and we had a little chat.

"I should have killed you that day when you gate-crashed my daughter's party."

"You should have. Now I'm going to haunt you for the rest of your life."

She smiled at me. It was a toothless sardonic smile devoid of any friendliness.

"You think you are clever right?"

"No I don't," I replied, "Jonasi approached me. He wooed me, and then screwed me. If there's anyone you ought to kill, it's him. He's the one at fault here. Don't fight with me, fight with him."

"You could have said no. You could have had the decency to keep your legs shut."

I looked her in the eyes and said, "If you were in my shoes would you have said no?"

I let the question linger in the air and it went unanswered. We stared at each other for a long time, evaluating one another. Sizing each other up like boxers in a knockout tournament. I decided then that I liked Joyce's mother. She had balls, extremely big ones like soccer balls. I even liked her quirky dress sense. She was swathed in a billowing caftan that had RG's face painted on it. Talk about undying, unwavering patriotism.

"So what did he promise you?" she asked.

"The world," I replied.

"Now I know you're not that stupid."

"I'm not," I replied, "But just so you know, he has paid *lobola* for me. My parents are happy. I'm happy."

"Welcome to the family," she replied drily.

"Thank you," I replied tartly, "I actually thought you would beat me. I guess you have better manners than your daughter."

"It's too late to give you a hiding," she sniggered. "Your parents should have done that a long time ago. Now we have to live with the mess."

She left then. I exhaled deeply. I spoke too soon. I don't think I like Joyce's mother after all. At least Joyce is an open book. That mother of hers is something else. I would not put it past her to get thugs to maul me to death. After her little visit I asked Jonasi to get security outside my door. Even when I went back home I insisted he post two guards at my gate.

"I told Joyce everything," Jonasi confessed.

"Which is good," I replied.

"I think you two need to try and coexist. You can't fight each other for the rest of your lives."

"That's true Jonasi. I think it's important that our kids know each other and respect each other."

He smiled and drew me into his arms and held me tight.

"You are such a wonderful person. I wish Joyce could be as understanding as you are."

My "understanding" paid off because Jonasi did not go home that night or the night after. A week passed, two weeks, three then a whole month. He was with me, helping me out with the girls. There was nothing sexual about his presence. I was in no condition to be having sex. I had stitches up to my arse. Even when I looked in the mirror I shuddered. My features were distorted and my body was disfigured. My breasts were like watermelons, seeping with milk. My belly button was having conversations with my cunt. Even with my pimpled face and disfigured nose Jonasi still looked at me like I was the most beautiful woman in the world. Others radiate with motherhood, I didn't. If anyone thought that Jonasi was in it for the sex they needed to rethink that because he was in it for the long haul. He loved me and my children. I was going to do everything in my power to legitimise my presence.

When the girls were six months old and I no longer looked like a car that needed panel beating, I had a "baby welcome party" for them. I invited Joyce but she did not attend. She sent presents though. A twin baby stroller from "Toys"Я"Us and lots of cuddly toys with the card signed "Love from the 1st family." When the girls turned one, I went crazy and threw a birthday party for them. I was now back to my old self, fitter and firmer than ever though my breasts had refused to shrink but I was okay with it, the girls were not the only ones who liked suckling on my breasts. I had the girls dressed in matching pink frocks with pink ribbons in their hair. I also wore a tiny off-the-shoulder pink dress and pink diamonds in my ears. We had a pink tent; pink-and-white tablecloths, pink-and-white roses and pink champagne. This time Joyce did show up at my house, wearing a white voile dress and plenty of gold. I had not seen Joyce since that time in hospital and I had to give credit to the enemy, she was really looking good. I had thought she would have withered under the stress this past year but she looked absolutely radiant. She was sporting a long weave, her skin glowing, fresh out of the beauty parlour. Her hands were perfectly manicured and so were her feet. She walked hand in hand with Shumi, who was also dressed in a white linen shirt and pants.

"Thanks for coming," I spoke, welcoming her to the party.

I did mean it. The last thing I wanted was for her to cause a scene at my perfect little pink party. I looked around for her mother. She would definitely have her boxing gloves on.

"Shumi's been dying to meet the girls," she replied cordially.

Her son ran off to get a glimpse of the girls who were perched in their pink baby high chairs.

I could see Joyce's eyes quickly scan the place, getting an eyeful of everything.

"You've really outdone yourself."

"Thank you. We Gomora women have to carry the name with pride."

She gave me a half-hearted smile. I knew we were at the point of negotiating some kind of truce. Look, there was no point in fighting anymore. We both loved the same man. We both made love to the same man. We both had borne children with the same man. Like it or not, Jonasi was our common denominator. She was not going anywhere and neither was I. There is a very simple theory in life, if you can't beat them, join them. Joyce had tried to beat me but had failed. Her only choice was to forge an alliance with me.

"Do you want to see the rest of the house?" I suggested.

She nodded and so I took her on the tour of my Ballantyne home, proudly showing off my décor and creativeness. At least she could see her husband's money was being well spent. She was full of compliments. When we returned outside we had a glass of champagne. Then one glass turned into three. Jonasi arrived around 3 p.m. to take pictures with the girls who cried instead of blowing out the lone candle on their shared birthday cake. The three of us posed for a portrait. Jonasi stood in the middle with his arms around us. Joyce left shortly afterwards with a bottle of champagne. Shumi stayed to play.

"I'm proud of you," said Jonasi, after Joyce had left.

"We are trying, I replied.

He took my hand and held it in his. We kissed right there and then, the sun beating down on our backs. And no, there were no frogs that turned into princes. Look this is not the fairy-tale ending you get in books but it was close. I had my perfect pink-coloured life.

twelve

I met Jonasi inside a crowded nightclub at 2 a.m. Normally, children my age are not allowed into night-clubs but how many clubs really enforce the No-Under-18 Rule? They just want to make money and don't give a hoot if they break the law in the process. I started clubbing when I was 15, started drinking when I was 14 and had my first sexual encounter when I was 12. You are probably thinking that "I like things". I didn't then. I was really innocent until one of the patrons at my mother's shebeen raped me. I could barely walk I was bleeding so much. When I told my mother she slapped me hard across the face and said:

"That man pays your school fees."

I hated school, hated it with a passion. So when I failed my "O" Levels it came as no surprise to anyone. I think I would have surprised myself if I had passed. My grandmother wanted me to repeat but my mother refused. She said she had no money to waste and told me to get a job. What kind of jobs do you get when you have no qualifications? The kind where you smile at the boss and he instantly likes you. I am extremely beautiful. I have the kind of looks that make people stop in the street and stare. For a long time I wished I was just a plain Jane because my looks just attracted the wrong kind of attention. I really don't know who I got my good looks from because my mother is a fat washed-out shebeen queen who's seen better days. I don't know who my father was. I don't even think my mother knows. I vowed to myself I would not turn out like my mother. So I made up my mind I would use my looks to better myself. And I did. I am one of those girls on the payroll who gets paid too much for doing too little. I mean come on, how difficult is manning a switchboard or being someone's glorified PA? I'm in between jobs at the moment. Rhino, my boyfriend, says I shouldn't work. Well that's okay, as long as he is giving me the money to pay my rent, buy my food, and get my hair and nails done. Rhino also gives me cab fare so that I can get round town. It would not do for my image to be jumping in and out of minibus taxis. Tito, my other boyfriend is like an insurance policy in case Rhino defaults on his obligations. They are both married but what they have in common is money and me of course. Except that they don't know about each other. Rhino is a businessman and Tito is a dealer. If Tito ever found about Rhino he would beat me to death. He's the possessive type. I don't think Rhino would care. He just wants me to be available to service his needs. Then when they are both unavailable I do have other men to tend to my needs. Like tonight, this guy called Farai offered to take me out. Who would say no to free dinner and free booze? It beats staying home and watching DSTV. I know at the end of the night Farai will want to sleep with me but its okay. All men want sex at the end of the day. The trick is to make sure that I get more than just an orgasm from it. My mother is always hounding me for money. If I tell her I don't have any she sends me on a guilt trip about the sacrifices she made for me. Like I asked to be born. Trust me, if it had been possible I would have aborted myself at birth. But I'm here now and I have to make the most of it. So where was I? Oh I was telling you about Jonasi. I was sitting at the bar drinking Johnny Walker Red (I graduated from ciders a long time ago) and he was standing at the other end of the bar. I had seen him checking me out a couple of times though I pretended not to notice. Jonasi is one of those middle-aged coons; you know the ones that try too hard. You've probably seen them at the club behaving like total assholes trying to dance to Jay Z. Okay, I'll hand it to Jonasi he had a certain coolness about him and a measure of dignity which escaped some of his peers. He sidled up to me and offered to buy me another round.

I looked him squarely in the eye and said, "Buy me the whole damn bottle."

He did not flinch and obliged me. First things first, I don't want a man with no cents near me. There will be no romance without finance. Call me a gold digger or a money monger, whatever, but I don't want a broke-ass nigger next to me. I have done broke. I know what it means to go to bed on an empty stomach. I know what it means to walk barefoot because your mother could not afford to buy you a pair of shoes. I know what it's like to ache for things you can't afford. That phase of my life has come and gone.

"So what's a gorgeous young woman like you doing sitting here alone?"

I rolled my eyes upwards. For a man dressed like him

I expected he would come up with a better come-on line. Honestly! Then again what can you expect from these fossils?

"I'm not alone," I replied, "My boyfriend is over there on the dance floor."

Farai was getting his groove on with a bevy of beauties. Farai is young and agile on his feet. He has a great body too and a tight ass unlike some of the fossils I go to bed with. Their asses are so wrinkled sometimes I have to ask myself if its flesh I'm holding onto or a mohair throw. Farai and I would make a nice couple. But Farai is still intent on sowing his wild oats. If it's not me on his arm, it's some other beauty. Then I ask myself if I want that headache of being in a monogamous relationship and clawing over one man. Despite this I want to be Farai's main chick. His wife even. Men will always cheat but I'd rather be somebody's wife than somebody's whore. I want the security that comes with marriage. The security of belonging...

"You are making a mistake with that young guy," the man said.

Now he wanted to act like the father I never had. Old men love to lecture. Just give him the platform and he starts shitting pearls of wisdom.

I laughed drily, "So you want me to make an even bigger mistake with you?"

"You wouldn't be. It would be the best decision of your life. If you change your mind, call me."

He reached into his jacket and slipped his business card into my gaping cleavage. I read his card and it had the usual list of credentials. I grabbed my eyeliner from my purse and wrote my number on the back of his card. Lindani. 0915453333. I had three other lines but that was the one he would be most likely to reach me on.

"If you want me, you call me."

I had been there and done that. You call a man and then have to spend five minutes reminding him where and how you met. No thanks. Let him have the burden of reminding me where I might have seen his old face.

"Thanks for the bottle."

"There's more where that came from."

"What? You own a distillery?"

He laughed, his eyes wrinkling at the sides. It hit me then that he was actually quite a good-looking old man.

"You're funny. I'll definitely call you."

Farai came back then. He was also extremely possessive. He wanted to act like he owned me but if I asked for money he would act like he had constipation. Some brothers out there are tighter than virgins. From the rapport that followed, it appeared that they knew each other. After Jonasi had gone, Farai turned to me and said, "Where do you know Jonasi from?"

"Who the hell is he?" I replied.

"He's one of the few rich black men in this country. He also happens to own the bank I work for."

I shifted in my seat. Money makes me wet. Farai went on to give me a blow-by-blow account of Jonasi and I suddenly wished I had taken his number. I would have definitely called his house down.

Jonasi did call me the next day and invited me out for dinner. I obviously said yes. I had to blow off Rhino and told him that my mother was around. Then Tito came by and started throwing his weight around. He left around 6 p.m. because his missus was threatening to can his balls if he did not come home within the hour. After he had gone, I bathed and dressed in a brand new frock that I had bought with Rhino's cash. Jonasi sent his driver to pick me up in a sleek SL500. He took me to La Mirabelle at the Meikles for dinner and he introduced me to Moët & Chandon. I was so bubbly and happy I thought I would burst. Most of the fossils I move around with don't wine and dine me. They just fuck me. Half the time they don't want to be seen with me in public. We might go to those out-of-town digs where people braai meat and grope in dark corners. Or worse still in some out-of-the-way obscure restaurant where you know you won't bump into anyone. But here was Jonasi, treating me like a princess. For those few hours I felt special. After he paid the whopping bill and tipped the waiter generously, we drove home. He did not insist on coming up but just thanked me for spending time with him.

"It's a pleasure," I replied, standing outside the car, the cool nippy breeze blowing against my legs.

Usually I have to fight men off at my doorstep, some even from my bed but here was Jonasi, cool as a cat just thanking me for a wonderful evening. This was definitely new to me. Then I started to panic. Maybe he did not find me attractive. Oh no, that would be an incredibly big loss. I had to do something. Jonasi was a big fish. I could not let him get away. Men like him only come around once in a lifetime.

I climbed back into the car and said to him, "I didn't thank you properly for tonight."

I reached for the zip of his trousers and wrapped my lips around his dick. I sucked on him like I was sucking on a lollipop. He was totally blown over as he came fast and hard. Then I left, knowing I had made a lasting impression on the man.

thirteen

What do you do when you discover your husband has children outside your marriage? Not one, not two but four? An affair is one thing but children are quite another. They are the evidence of that betrayal, living proof of a philandering husband who has not only sown his seed, but firmly planted it in some woman's womb. I could have dealt with one child. If he had been apologetic, claimed it had been a mistake I would have forgiven him. I would have even gone as far as embracing that kid into our lives. But how the hell do you deal with four kids? I had my four then there were four more kids out there. Jonasi had grown from being a father of four to a father of eight. To think he was pestering me to have another one then there would have been nine. Nine little Gomora kids. I was glad I had my tubes tied. It was the best thing I had ever done. Here I was thinking I had sole rights to being the mother of Jonasi's children. I thought it gave me the upper hand. What a load of bollocks that was. There were other women out there walking with their chests pushed out saying they had mothered Jonasi's kids. I actually felt disgusted. Disgusted to be a part of that brigade. So disgusted that I got violently sick. I threw up in disgust. The vile contents spewed out of me like a fountain that my mother warned me I would vomit my heart and lungs out at the rate I was going. She had no idea that I actually wanted to lose my heart. If only the meaty pieces of my broken heart could emerge in the stream of bile then I would flush it down the loo. You don't need a heart to deal with this kind of confusion. A heart had no place there. Yes, that's what I was in, a mess. My mother was by my side, holding my hand again. Jonasi was nowhere in sight. The minute the histrionics had started he had run off to his mistress again. He'd gone to hide out in paradise, leaving me to deal with the bullshit. Yes. That's exactly what it was, bullshit. He accused me of falling apart yet he was the biggest instigator of my unhappiness.

"She must be good in bed," my mother kept saying.

"And I'm not?" I replied, bent over double over the toilet seat, my mother holding on to my weave.

"What else can I say? She has to have something going for her. If it's not on her face then it has to be in her pants."

"He says he loves her."

My mother had no clever jibe for that one and that made me cry even more. My husband told me point blank that he loves another woman.

"And me? Do you love me Jonasi?"I had cried out.

"Yes Joyce. I love you very much. That's why I'm still here."

"But you promised me you had ended it with her. You promised Jonasi!"

"I tried Jo but I couldn't stay away. I can't live without her. She makes my blood rush!"

"And I make it curdle? Is that it?"

"Joyce you don't understand. I love you both. You give me different things. Why can't you understand that?"

"Because I can't. You are supposed to love me and me alone. You swore before God to forsake all others."

"Don't be selfish Joyce. There's enough love to go around."

"Ah yes, Jonasi, and you are giving out the love aren't you? They must be lining up to get pregnant!"

"Look Joyce if you are not willing to have my children, other women will. I told you I wanted another child but instead you go and get your bloody tubes tied. I told you I wanted six kids. Now I have them. "

I was stunned. I felt like Jonasi had punched me in the stomach but he had not even laid a finger on me. I wanted to double over the pain was so bad. You know I thought I would never feel so much pain again but this was even worse than the affair. I can't even describe to you how I felt. I literally dropped to my knees and cried.

"Joyce pull yourself together!"

That made me cry even harder. He was so cold and aloof. If there was something I could not understand about Jonasi was his ability to switch on and off like a light bulb. How could he stand there with no emotion and tell me that he had children with another woman like it did not matter and that I should just pull myself together? The condescending asshole.

"Mummy are you okay?" I heard Shumi's voice.

He was standing in the doorway his face crumpled in fright.

"She's fine," replied Jonasi dismissively. "Go to your room. Your mother is fine."

Then he turned his attention to me, "Joyce get it together," he admonished. "You are upsetting the kids."

"Whilst we're on the subject Jonasi, are there any other kids I should know about?"

I don't even know why I asked that question but it just slipped out. We had talked about the twins so we might as well do an inventory of all the other children.

"There are," he replied, "I have another son and daughter. They live with their mother."

I was speechless. You know raging denial would have sufficed but he stood there and told me without flinching that he had two more children. That was the final arrow through my heart.

"It's nothing for you to worry about Joyce. Just pull yourself together."

He walked out of our bedroom. I heard the footfall as he made his way downstairs. In the distance I could hear him rev his engine. He was gone. It felt like déjà vu. We had been down this road before; I could not believe I was back in this place again. Then as I lay there in a heap I realised that we had not really moved from it. This was the stuff that was revolving around my head over and over again. Now are you even surprised why I was sick?

I got well. I had to. There are just so many nervous breakdowns you can have in one lifetime. Then I had to go through the rigmarole of explaining Jonasi's disappearance to Rudo when she came home over the weekend.

"He's over at Matipa's," I replied. "You can go and visit him there. You also have twin sisters now."

Why lie? If we were all going to live open and honest lives I needed to start being honest with myself and honest with the children. She was shocked. Matipa's name had not been spoken in this house in a long time.

"But I thought it was over...." she mumbled.

"It's not Rudo. Your father loves her very much. Now they have babies."

"Why can't we be a normal family?" she cried out. "Why can't we be normal?"

I shrugged my shoulders. I could not answer her. When I got married all I had wanted for us was to have a normal family life with a mother and father and the children; the normal family life that I had grown up in. My mother had successfully managed to shield us from the vagaries of life. I mean we grew up thinking our father was a fucking saint only to discover he was no better than the rest of them. Maybe the abnormal was very normal. How did I even begin to explain it? How could I tell her that normal things did not excite her father?

"So are you and Daddy going to get divorced?"

I could see the panic and anxiety all over her face.

"I don't know," I replied.

That was the honest truth. Just a few days ago we had grown from a family of four kids to eight. I was still trying to deal with that. Actually the more I thought about, the idea emerged to throw a party and invite all of Jonasi's kids and their mothers so we could all sit around the bonfire swapping stories about Daddy. Yes, that's what he had reduced us to. That is what he had reduced my life to, a mockery. So shoot me if I didn't have any brilliant ideas about what to do next. I had not thought that far. All Jonasi could tell me was to pull myself together. There was no talk of divorce, yet. So I was not wrong to say I didn't know.

"What do you know, Mum? What do you know?"

"I know for sure that your dad has eight kids, you included. He has other women in his life who he says he loves. I know that for sure. That's what I know."

She stared back at me with tears in her big brown eyes.

"I'm never coming home again," she replied.

"Don't," I said, "Don't come home if you don't want to."

She ran out of my bedroom crying. Selfish bitch. She thought this was easy for me; it wasn't. I was hurting too and, no, I did not have all the answers. There were no manuals for this kind of thing. I had combed the Bible looking for verses to deal with this and I could not find any. The Old Testament was rife with polygamous marriages: Leah, Rachel, Bathsheba… I could go on but none of the verses delved into their emotions. There was no discussion on how to cope in such instances. And here I was, caught up in the middle of it.

Rudo finally came home when the schools closed. I still had no answers. Jonasi had not come back home either. Anyway I decided I was not going to sit around and wait for him to come back from his little sojourn at Matipa's. I took my mother, Rudo and the boys and we flew to London. I just needed time out. The minute Tino laid eyes on me he knew that all was not well at home. We sat up all night talking (me crying) about his father's shenanigans. He said it would be alright, that it would blow over but deep down I knew nothing would ever be alright again. After London we flew to visit my sister in America. She was adamant that I should divorce Jonasi and when I left for home two weeks later I was also convinced it was the right thing to do. We spent a weekend in South Africa visiting Jennifer. She was sympathetic but insisted I hang in there and spend the bastard's money. Trust me I had shopped those past four weeks; shopped till I dropped to my knees in exhaustion. But let me tell you something, no Prada gown or Chanel jacket in the world would have given me the peace of mind I so desperately craved. All the Jimmy Choos in the world would not have mended my broken insides. When the boutiques closed I lay awake at night crying. I looked glorious on the outside but on the inside I was slowly dying.

Jonasi came to pick us up at the airport the day we arrived. He said he was happy to see me feeling stronger. Then he started telling me about the twins. How fast they were growing. I tell you if anyone had asked me when I started hating Jonasi it was then. I hated him with my entire being. I could not even bring myself to look at him. I wanted to hurt him, physically hurt him. That's how much hate I felt towards him. He had belittled my dreams, belittled everything I believed in. Most of all he had belittled me. He said he loved me but Jonasi did not love anyone. He was incapable of it. He only loved himself. That night he even tried to make love to me but I froze. His touch made my insides go cold. I could not even turn around to face him. He gave up trying to stroke me up and get me in the mood.

"Maybe you need a bit more time," he said.

I knew I was never going to be ready.

"I still love you and I want us to be a family. We can all be a family."

I turned to face him then.

"I want a divorce, Jonasi."

"No Joyce," he replied, "I love you and I'm not going to divorce you. The only time you are going to stop being my wife is when I leave this house in a coffin. When I said my vows I meant it. Till death do we part, Joyce."

I wanted to spit in his face but instead I gave him my back. I felt the tears roll down my cheeks. Now he wanted to hold me ransom to this marriage? This was even worse than being raped. And I was being raped from behind.

fourteen

I was feeling all loved up and happy lying in Farai's arms when Jonasi called. When I saw his name I almost jumped out of my skin. I had him saved as "Uncle Joe" so that Farai would not get suspicious when he went scrolling through my phone. I crawled out of bed and went into the shower. I let the water run so that he could not hear anything of my conversation.

"Hi Jonasi."

"Hello my apple tart," replied Jonasi.

I don't know what it is about old fossils and their choice of using food as endearments. Nonetheless I played along. With the kind of money Jonasi gave me I would lick his balls and chew them if I had to.

"Sugar pie, I've been missing you terribly!"

"So have I. Are you able to take some time off work? I want you to come to Johannesburg with me."

I screamed in delight, "Oh yes I can."

I would quit my job if I had to. Not really, I would just call in sick. Who in their right mind would turn down an opportunity to go to Johannesburg? Definitely not me.

"Get ready and I'll have my driver pick you up at 11 a.m. I have a 3 o'clock meeting there and I've decided to spend the weekend playing golf."

"I'll be ready." I said.

He hung up then and just as you know it the door opened then and Farai walked in. I wondered if he had heard anything. He still looked sleepy eyed.

"Don't tell me you're showering without me."

"I'm not," I replied.

We got into the water together and I gave him a blow job. That really woke him up. Afterwards I made him breakfast before getting dressed myself. You see when I'm at Farai's place I try to act like wifey so that he can see me in that role. I even cook supper, clean after him and do his laundry. I am really campaigning hard to be his missus. I guess you are wondering why I don't just fall pregnant and fast-track my way into his life? Trust me I have tried that. He made me have an abortion. He said he would have a child when he was good and ready. When he dropped me off at work he asked me if I would be coming back to his place. I said I would, knowing only too well that I would be in Johannesburg that evening. I spent an hour at work before feigning sickness, then I went to get my hair done. I called Farai from the salon and told him my mother was sick and that I had to travel to Bulawayo. He was sympathetic and offered to fly me down. I told him it was alright and that I was already on the bus to Bulawayo.

"I'll put some money into your account. To cover any expenses."

"Thanks baby," I replied.

Farai was slowly starting to let loose with the purse strings. Sometimes I wonder if I am making a big mistake wanting to be tied down to a man as stingy as Farai. But you know lately he has started talking serious stuff. He wants me to move in with him but I have told him he has to pay first. Until then I was still servicing Tito, Rhino, Jonasi, Edgar, Leonard and anyone else who is willing to give me a dime.

We flew to Johannesburg first class baby. And I acted like the first-class whore that I was. We were chauffeur driven to the Michelangelo Hotel in Sandton. We checked in as "Mr and Mrs Gomora" though the way the receptionist looked at us I could tell she was not fooled one bit. It looked more like Mr Gomora and his daughter. Jonasi left me to lie in and order room service whilst he rushed off to his meeting. I needed to get my strength back after a night with Farai. He was a stallion in bed. We have mad sexual chemistry together. I actually think Farai is falling in love with me. I am in love with him and I swear to God I will stop all this shit if he puts a ring on my finger. Like now that I'm gone I know he's probably shagging the whole of Harare. That's what saddens me. I don't want to be the other woman in a man's life. There's no pension in this life. One day I will get old and no man will want me so I need to get a life policy now and that's marriage. When Jonasi returned from his meeting I was ready for him. He would have been a good candidate for marriage but he made it crystal clear to me that's he's not in the market for a wife. He told me he had three wives and that he was happily married to all three of them. He is full of himself. Did he honestly think I wanted to be wife number four? I know I am a wild cannon but even I have standards. I am happy being one of Jonasi's girlfriends. I know I am one of many. You see Jonasi can disappear for months on end and you won't hear from him. Then from nowhere he'll pop out of the blue and expect you to drop everything for him. I do because even though Jonasi disappears, his money doesn't. Every month I get an allowance from him. So yes when he calls I make sure I drop everything for him, my pants included and I shag him like there's no tomorrow. I always make sure our encounters are memorable. That was what I was doing now. I was straddling him, bouncing up and down on his firm dick. For a man his age he could actually keep it hard. I was impressed. I had slept with some men who could only stay semi-hard, but Jonasi could still hold his own. I increased the tempo, causing him to grunt in ecstasy. I could tell he was about to come and his groans were getting louder and louder. Then I felt him come. His body stiffened as he exploded inside me like a volcano. I collapsed onto his chest, which was wet with his sweat. I lay on top of him, his deflating penis still lodged inside of me. I loved the sensation of being next to him. We lay there for a long time, no words being spoken. I was already thinking of what to do to him next but I figured he would be out of action.

"That was amazing," spoke Jonasi, breaking the silence, "I had almost forgotten how good you are in bed."

"Well I'm here to remind you," I replied.

I kissed him tenderly, moving my groin in circular motions. He slapped me gently on the buttocks, "Now let's shower and get something to eat. I'm totally finished."

I slid off his slippery wet body and made my way into the shower. I could feel his semen trickling down my thighs. Jonasi and I don't use condoms. I only use condoms with men who insist, and trust me, most of them don't.

We had an intimate dinner at the resplendent "Butcher Shop and Grill" on Nelson Mandela Square. I tried not to flinch at the price tag that came attached to some of those meals. He ordered a bottle of pinotage and I drank it like I had been born drinking red wine. After dinner he suggested we go dancing and he took me to Club Kilimanjaro. I tell you that place took nightclubbing to another level with its spacious dance floors and stylish bars. The atmosphere was electric and vibrant. The music pulsated around us and the energy flowed between us. We only got back to the hotel room at 4 a.m. and tumbled into bed. I was all fired up but after finishing a bottle of Glenfiddich whiskey Jonasi failed to launch. So we slept and woke up at midday and had breakfast in bed. In the afternoon Jonasi went to play golf with some business colleagues. He gave me money to go shopping in Sandton. I shopped till a line of sweat formed on my brow. I left no shop un-entered. I got back to the hotel well after 6 p.m. my arms laden with bags. I could have shopped all night, it's just that the money had run out. Jonasi laughed at me when he saw me snowed under the Aldo, Stuttafords, Spitz and Levis bags.

"That reminds me. I need to get stuff for my concubines. I'll just get them perfume at the airport."

We freshened up and then went to have dinner at Wang Thai. I let Jonasi order for me as I was not familiar with Thai food. He was really showing me the finer things in life. This is the kind of life I hoped to have with Farai.

"So Jonasi," I asked, "Do you ever take your wives on business trips?"

"I do," replied Jonasi, "When they want to come."

I could not figure out why anyone would say "no" to spending days in a fancy hotel and shopping your head off.

"My wives only come when it's New York or Brazil. I

guess Johannesburg is too low class for them. But I'm sure Essie would come. Of all my wives she's the most down to earth. I'll probably bring her next time. Our daughter will be starting university here."

Every time he started speaking of his children, I would be reminded how old Jonasi was. One thing for sure, was this man loved his children and made sure they were well taken care of. I had considered having a baby with Jonasi if things didn't work out with Farai. At least that way I'd know I'd be set for life. But I had to tread carefully. For all you know Jonasi might just march me off to the abortion clinic as well.

"What's Essie like?" I asked.

I was curious about Jonasi's wives. I knew I would never meet them but there was no harm in asking.

"Essie is the fattest of all my wives. She wasn't always fat. She used to be like you. Actually you kind of remind me of her in a way."

I don't know if that was a good thing or a bad thing.

"Joyce is the most beautiful of the three. She has class. Joyce polished me into the black diamond I am. I used to be rough around the edges."

He laughed at his own joke and l laughed with him.

"And Matipa?"

I knew about Matipa because she called a lot and he would say that was Matipa.

"Ahh Matipa. She's not a conventional beauty. There's something unique and interesting about her. Very intelligent girl. There are not many smart women out there but she's sharp. She'll do great things in life."

I was afraid to ask about me. What was his take on me? Anyway it did not matter. I was there to enjoy Jonasi and all he had to offer.

fifteen

Ever heard the phrase sleeping with the enemy? That's exactly what I was doing. On one side of the bed there was Matipa, with Jonasi on the other. We had formed an alliance of sorts, something like Mussolini and Hitler. My mother told me to keep my friends close but my enemies closer. She said it was always good to keep abreast of what the enemy was doing. And so I did. On some weekends Matipa brought the twins to play and on others I left Shumi there to play. That's how I got wind of the fact that Matipa was driving a Grand Cherokee Jeep so I told Jonasi I wanted to be upgraded to a black shiny BMW X5. He obliged me. I also decided to get new rings whilst we were at it. At that point in time I think Jonasi would have given me a slice of the moon if he could. He thought because I was now on talking terms with Matipa I was okay with everything he was doing. As far he was concerned he was having his cake, eating it and shitting it. I was certain if he could, Jonasi would not have minded having Matipa and me in the same bed having wild orgies. The only thing that prevented him from living out his fantasy was the fact that I still withheld sex from him. I told him point blank that he could have sex with Matipa until his dick fell off because Joyce General Dealers no longer stocked that commodity. He tried to force me a couple of times but when he realised just how disinterested and apathetic I was he stopped trying. Passive resistance I called it. He was convinced I would come around.

"When you miss me you'll know where to find me."

What he did not know was the thought of having sex with him filled me with revulsion. Our lovemaking no longer inspired warm fuzzy feelings, it just repulsed me. The thought of him dipping into another woman's pussy then dipping into mine was enough to put anyone off sex. I didn't know the names of his other paramours (I didn't want to know them) but I knew that I did not want to be poked by the same dick. He was painting us with the same filthy brush.

"He's going to die of Aids," my mother said.

"And you'll die with him," said my sister pointedly.

It was one of those rare occasions when Jennifer had come to Zimbabwe to visit. The last time she visited was when Daddy died. My sister acted more South African than the South Africans themselves.

"Why are you even sticking around? This country has gone to the dogs!" she moaned.

Jennifer moaned about everything. She complained that there was no fuel, no electricity, no Sandton City and Fourways Crossing.

"Some of us have a life here," I responded defensively.

"What life Joyce? You live with Father Zimbabwe who's going to give you Aids."

"And you think you are immune?" said my mother coming to my defence, "Look for all you know Joyce could be

HIV positive but there's no use being pessimistic. We all survive by the grace of God. As long as you have a man in your life you are at risk."

The last time I had an HIV test was when I was pregnant with Shumirai. Then I had gone boldly marching into the doctor's office with nothing to fear. Now I was shit-scared of having my blood drawn because it was pretty obvious my husband did not use condoms. He only dived in his birthday suit. What guarantee did I have that his other floozies were faithful? What did they do on those nights when Jonasi had flashbacks of his past life and decided that he wanted to wake up in his Glen Lorne home next to his Glen Lorne wife?

"You know I would get a divorce if he would agree."

"If you really wanted to leave him you would," snickered my sister. "Just pack your bags and come and live with me. He'll grant you a divorce on the grounds of desertion."

"Joyce is not going anywhere," crowed my mother. "If there's anyone leaving that house it will be Jonasi, in a coffin."

"So what does Joyce do now? Sit it out until he drops dead? What if he doesn't?"

"You just need to do something with your life Joyce. Something to take your mind off this," countered my mother. "Life doesn't revolve around Jonasi and his millions."

That's when I decided to go back to school. I had my "O" Level certificate so I decided to do my "A" Levels. So I registered at Speciss College and became a student. The only good thing is that I did not have to wear a uniform. I chose the same subjects that Rudo was doing: accounting, maths and business management. Nowadays Rudo and I had very little in common. If anything, we fought a lot, so the best I could for us was to find common ground on the school front. At least I could bully her into doing my assignments when I felt lazy. Tino was very encouraging and told me repeatedly that he was proud of me. That alone spurred me on to keep going to classes. Trust me I was very aware of the fact that I was the oldest in my class, that I was also the only one who drove a BMW X5 to school. I was even older than some of my teachers, except one. His name was Stanslous Denga of the Denga, Hikwa and Partners firm. He taught for free as a way of giving back to the community. He was a good teacher and very handsome in a distinguished sort of way. Think Denzel Washington. (Look I already had Blair Underwood at home and what good did that do me.) Stanslous was passionate about teaching. He was always prepared and went the extra mile. He really motivated me to do well in accounting. I sat at the front of the class and paid a lot of attention to him, the way he spoke, the way he dressed. I was determined to pass all my tests and worked extra hard. I could afford to read well into the night now that I was a black widow. On the few nights that Jonasi was home he did not expect any marital favours from me. One night he woke up and asked me what I was doing.

"Trying to study," I told him.

"You know when you said you were going to school I didn't think you were serious."

"I am Jonasi. Very serious."

We ended up sitting the whole night doing maths equations. I discovered Jonasi was actually a much better teacher than Stanslous. He had a way of explaining things in such simplistic terms that I understood. By the time the sun came up I realised that I had spent a glorious morning with the old Jonasi that I used to know and love.

I almost had tears in my eyes to think that this is what we had come to. What had happened to us?

"Don't worry Jo. You'll pass," he said cupping my chin playfully.

"Thanks for the vote of confidence."

He kissed me then. I kissed him back. I realised then how much I really missed him. We fell back onto the bed. His kisses were like Godiva chocolates melting in your mouth. I felt his hands stroke my silky thighs and it seemed like I was on fire. Then I had visions of other women swooning as Jonasi kissed them and just like that the spell was broken. I pulled away as abruptly as if I had tasted poison.

"I need to get Shumi ready for school."

"I'll take him," he volunteered.

"I need to get ready for school."

I jumped out of bed and headed straight into the shower. I did not have my first class until 10 a.m., but I did not want to sit around and test my immunity to Jonasi's touch.

My business studies lecture was over by 12 p.m. and my next class was at four. It gave me enough time to pick up Shumi. He was the only one at home these days. Now that Garikai was in Form 1 we had him in boarding school like Rudo. The only child that needed any babying was Shumi. We went home, had lunch and I helped him with his homework. By the time I left for my evening classes he was already seated in front of the television watching Cartoon Network. Accounting was my last class for the day and I had received a terribly low mark for my last assignment. I was literally crushed because I thought I had done well. Stanslous asked me to stay back at the end of the class. I felt even more embarrassed because

I was the only person who had failed the assignment. He told me not to worry as he gave me a blow-by-blow account as to where I had erred. By the time we were done it was almost 7 p.m.

"Sorry to keep you late, you probably have to cook supper for the family."

"Not even," I replied, "I might even get a pizza on my way home."

Now that Jonasi was a rolling stone and most of the children were away I did not kill myself making three-course dinners anymore. The maid cooked for Shumi and if Jonasi happened to roll by he would have to eat whatever was there.

"Well if you don't mind, maybe we can grab something to eat together."

I eyed him quizzically, "You don't want to piss off your wife. I'm sure she's set aside some supper for you."

"I don't have a wife, Joyce."

"What happened to her?"

"Let's get something to eat and I'll tell you all about it."

So we had dinner at the Blue Banana in the Avenues. It was awesome Thai food and we had equally awesome conversation. Just like my husband, Stanslous was a self-made millionaire. He also had the same rags-to-riches story to tell. It turns out he was in his fourth year when Jonasi was in his second year at university.

"Now my firm audits his firm. How ironic is that?"

I smiled, "Life is full of ironies."

"Now I'm auditing his wife. So tell me, who is Joyce?"

I shrugged my shoulders. There was nothing to tell really. I went to school. Met Jonasi, got married and had four kids. In a sentence that was my life punctuated with bullshit in the later years.

"You know being a homemaker is not a bad thing at all. Look you've paid your dues on the home front. Your children are all grown up now and there's nothing to stop you from pursuing your dreams."

"I don't even know what my dreams are, Stan, but what I know now is that I'm enjoying this. I really want to pursue accounting. Before I could not even read the balance sheet of J&J. Now I can. Now it makes sense. I really want to get involved."

"So pursue it Joyce. If you are really serious about it I can offer you a place to do articles at my firm. Pass your "A" Levels and I'll take you on."

I really got excited then and my eyes lit up and sparkled like the diamonds on my fingers.

"You could actually do articles anywhere really. Even the big four. You are a smart girl, Joyce. Don't underestimate yourself. Yes, you made some silly mistakes in your assignment, but I know you can do it."

I had never thought about having a career before but here was this man telling me that I could have one and that it was not too late. For a long time I thought that my life as I knew it was over and it was. The good thing was I could start over. It did not matter how old I was. This was something I could do without Jonasi. This was something I could do for myself. For me.

"I'm sure you could even do training in your husband's firm."

I held up my hands in protest, "I don't want to train under Jonasi. I want to do this for myself."

Stanslous looked at his watch, "It's late. I'm sure Jonasi won't appreciate me keeping his wife out so late."

"I don't think Jonasi cares," I replied, "That's the problem with you men. You make money and then you think you have the right to abuse everybody's feelings."

"Don't point fingers, women are just as bad!"

"That's not true Stan. I have done so much for Jonasi and he thanks me by sleeping with anything and everything."

"But you women do the same," he countered.

I was outraged. How could he sit there and say that? I had been faithful. In all my married life I had been faithful. Not once had I fluttered an eyelid at another man. Then again what did I expect? Stanslous was a man and he probably ran around just as much, if not twice as much, as Jonasi.

"Well what can you say?" I retorted.

"A lot actually. My wife of 15 years had more game than a soccer team. She used to cheat on me like there was no tomorrow. She was probably cheating on me even before we said 'I do' but I never saw it. I think I just chose to ignore it. Then she started to do it in my face and I could not ignore it. You know I got so desperate I even had her followed. You know I begged and pleaded with her to stop but that made her cheat even more. So I know what I'm talking about Joyce. I know what it feels like to lie awake at night waiting for someone to come home and they don't."

"So what happened? Did you divorce her?"

"No. Actually the more she cheated, the more I wanted her. It was sad. I was one sad guy. I think at the back of my mind I kept telling myself that one day she would change. That she would get tired of the game and that we would have a normal marriage. She didn't. She left me. She had everything, that woman, but she left it all to take off with some hobo. She woke up one morning and threw her ring in my face. The only consolation is she left me with the kids. Sometimes I look at those kids and wonder if they are even mine. But I don't want to know either. I think that would finish me. We've been divorced for five years now. She's in London. In those five years she has never bothered to see the kids. She'll call on their birthdays but that's it."

I was totally shocked. Why would any woman want to cheat on Stanslous? He looked like he was the perfect gentleman.

"So are you seeing anyone now?"

"I was. We broke up because she was tired of waiting for me to pop the question. I've done the marriage thing and it's enough. I'm leaving it to my kids. I don't think I can take that kind of abuse again."

I exhaled noisily. I was not the only one who walked around lugging a broken heart. However I looked at Stanslous and felt sad. I did not want to be like that five years from now. I wanted to be happy.

"Stan you owe it to yourself to be happy. You deserve to be happy."

"Can I?"

And unexpectedly he broke down and cried. I reached out and touched his hand in the dimly lit restaurant. He was a broken soul like me. Through no fault of our own we had been betrayed. We might have been down but we were not out. I'd be damned if I was going to spend the rest of my life being a sorry soul. I told myself then that I was going to be happy. Even if it killed me I was going to at least die trying to be happy. Without any hope I was no better than a dead person and as long as I was alive I owed it to myself to try.

sixteen

It was Jonasi's 41st birthday. I had sent him an sms to wish him well. He surprised me when he sms'ed back and said he would be coming over to my place in the next hour or two. I literally jumped out of bed because he was not even on the list of persons I expected to see today. I would have to take a bath. I had not bathed in days. Sometimes I was just too lazy to get up and bath. Especially if I was not going anywhere. However with Sarah around these days I was up and about. Even on those days I did not want to get up Sarah would come into my bedroom and we would watch movies all day. When she got bored with being around the house she would drive off into town and meet her uppity friends for a movie and coffee. Sometimes I look at Sarah and I am amazed that I gave birth to her. She is really beautiful. She's tall and dark skinned like her father. She is the female version of Jonasi. The beauty of it is that my daughter is not even aware of her good looks. She's still very playful and can be extremely childish. I was surprised when she told me she had a boyfriend. Some white boy called Herman. He is the son of the German ambassador. I have invited Herman around to the house a couple of times. He looks harmless and they play silly games together. It's a relationship I want to nurture. From a young age I had told Sarah never to look at township boys as anything more than friends. I told her there was nothing wrong with growing up in the township and she should never be ashamed of it but I also made it very clear she did not have to die here. So she grew up with the best of both worlds and that kept her grounded.

"Sarah," I said peeping around her bedroom door, "Could you bake a cake for your father? He's coming round."

Sarah literally jumped out of bed.

"Is daddy celebrating his birthday with us?" asked Sarah.

"I guess so," I replied.

"Yippee," she screamed.

Sarah raced to the kitchen and got busy. She worships the ground Jonasi walks on. Her loyalty to her absentee father always amused me but I figured it was a good thing she had Jonasi as her role model. And Jonasi had never let her down. He was there for her prize-giving ceremonies, parents' day and any other occasion when his presence was called for. You are probably wondering how Jonasi did the balancing act. Well none of his children went to the same schools at the same time. Sarah had been schooled at Arundel whilst Rudo was at Chisipite. Garikai was at St Georges and Blessing was at St Johns. Tino was at university in London and my daughter Sarah would be going to East London. None of the children were aware of the others' existence. I told Sarah and Blessing that they had other brothers and sisters and that one day they would meet. Whether it was at Jonasi's graveside or somewhere else one thing for sure was they were going to meet.

I decided I would cook trotters for Jonasi over an open fire. So I called Freedom and asked him to get some firewood and light me a fire. We don't stay with Freedom but he lives two blocks away with my parents. They took him in when he was 10 because Jonasi did not trust him around Sarah. I did not trust Freedom either. He was my son but he was a thug. He dropped out of school at sixteen so he could roam the streets sniffing glue and doing petty crime. Now at 26 he's graduated to car-jacking and smoking *mbanje*. I think Freedom will be dead by the time he hits 30. I know it's a cruel thing to say but I can just see it. People like him don't live long. I heard him arrive in his battered blue VW Golf. He was playing loud music as usual. He stank of cheap alcohol and looked like he had not slept in days.

"Is the big *dhara* coming?" he asked.

"Yes," I replied.

"You should be ashamed of yourself," he said. "After all these years and you are still servicing that *dhara*."

"Freedom light the fire and then piss off," I replied crisply.

Freedom had always been a difficult child. I used to *klap* him silly when he was younger. Now he throws his weight around and wants to *klap* me. He is also very judgemental. He calls me a whore whenever it suits him yet he still has the nerve to ask me for money. I guess the mistake I made with Freedom was he used to bear witness to my shenanigans. He saw me being picked up by other men. He saw me being shagged by other men. He saw things that he should never have seen as a child. That is why I changed my modus operandi when Sarah and Blessing were young. If I had any miscellaneous activities I wanted to engage in I made sure to do this outside my house and far from their innocent eyes. I also started going to church so that they would grow up in the spirit knowing full well the difference between good and evil and hopefully not get their wires crossed between the two.

"Where's Blessing?" he asked me. "Why doesn't he make the fire?"

"Blessing is still asleep," I replied but my youngest son could not make a fire to save his life.

"That fucking moffie. You are going to raise a moffie."

Strangely Freedom and Blessing got along very well. However I know my older son is poison and I'm afraid he'll turn Blessing into a miniature thug. Blessing is at that impressionable age when he wants to try out everything that's bad and Freedom wants to humour him. Whereas he and Sarah just don't see eye to eye. After he had got the fire up and running, Freedom put a loving arm around me and asked me for money. I gave him $300 just to get him out of my hair. He looked at me in with pure unadulterated loathing on his face.

"Is this all?"

"Go and get a job!" I hissed.

"You don't work, why should I?" he berated.

"Fuck off," I told him. "Just fuck off."

He brings out the worst in me. I looked up at the kitchen window and hoped Sarah had not heard me. The mother she knew was soft spoken and did not spit such bile from her mouth.

Freedom could sense my discomfort and leaned closer to me and whispered in my ear.

"Go and fuck Jonasi and then give me proper money."

He threw the money into the fire and walked off. I stood with my hands on my hips staring after him. The things we give birth to.

Jonasi arrived a little after midday. The main meal was a delectable pork-trotter stew which I served with creamy spinach in peanut-butter sauce, butternut and steaming hot *sadza* with the lingering smell of fire. Jonasi sang my praises throughout the lunch telling Sarah how well I cooked. For dessert, Sarah and Blessing brought him the cake which had 41 written in whipped cream. They sang for him and I could tell Jonasi was touched, really touched. He rewarded their efforts with money. That was the only way Jonasi could show his appreciation, with money. Sarah and Blessing said they were off to Avondale to spend it.

"Make sure you are home by six," he ordered.

I don't even think they heard him as they were already out the door. Then Jonasi turned to me and barked relentlessly about how he did not want Sarah staying out late at night.

"Sarah never stays out late," I replied defensively.

"She better not. I don't want to hear that nonsense Essie. Kids should not be given too much freedom. They go out late and dance their lives away in night clubs. Next thing you know she'll be pregnant. I don't want Sarah hanging around with boys either!"

"Jonasi, she's 19 not nine. She's obviously going to talk to boys."

"Sarah if I even hear about a boy in Sarah's life I'll beat you both. I am not paying school fees so that Sarah can major in boys."

I turned to my side and expelled a deep noisy breath. The last thing I needed from Jonasi was a lecture on how to raise kids. I had literally raised those children alone and now he wanted to lay down the law on how they would and would not behave.

"Look Jonasi," I snapped, "I think I've done a pretty good job so far. A mere thank you would suffice."

He could tell I was annoyed and put his arm around me. I threw it off abruptly.

"Sorry Essie, I just worry about her. She's my eldest daughter and I want to marry her off to a decent man. I don't want any funny stories with her."

"You mean like me?"

"I didn't say that."

"Look Jonasi we've all made mistakes and I know mine."

I stood up to clear the plates. I marched off into the kitchen and dumped them in the sink. I was running the water when I heard Jonasi's voice.

"Essie can you leave the plates for a minute?"

And do what? Sit and listen to his bullshit. Then I felt his hands around my thick waist.

"Essie," he murmured into my ear, "I said I'm sorry."

He kissed me tenderly on the side of my neck.

"Can we just forget about the plates and go out somewhere. You know Essie, you haven't danced for me in a long time. I miss the way you dance."

I giggled. I am not one to hold grudges. He hugged me tighter, burying his face into my back.

"Come on. Let's go dancing then."

We took off in Jonasi's new shiny gold Land Cruiser. He said he was taking me to a friend's farm on the outskirts of Murewa. It was quite a drive and I wondered if Jonasi would be back in town in time.

"Isn't Joyce throwing you a surprise party?" I asked.

For his 40th she had thrown Jonasi a huge party at Leopard Rock. The party had started on a Friday and ended on a Sunday. Jonasi had invited me, Wonder, Gershom and their wives. Joyce had us seated at a table together at the back of the room. We were her husband's poor trashy relatives. She called me *Tete* Essie and never even gave me a second look. It did not bother me. I knew my place. In our little corner we watched her prance around with her uppity attitude and her nose in the air. Matipa (we called her *mainini*) was also there too. She looked very disinterested and sat at a table surrounded by men, drinking red wine and smoking a thick Cuban cigar. Anyway we had fun on Jonasi's 40th. We ate, drank and were extremely merry. Wonder got so drunk he shat himself. I was so drunk I had to be carried to my room. You can rest assured Joyce would not be inviting us to any more parties.

"This year things are rough my dear. Joyce didn't even wish me happy birthday. I had to remind her that it's my birthday. Even Shumi didn't make me a card this year. Tino normally calls me on my birthday but this year there was nothing. As for Rudo, I had to call her and then she says 'sorry Daddy, happy birthday'. Garikai could not care less whose birthday it was. You know Essie that boy has a sick attitude. He's like Freedom. I'd like to beat the hell out of him one of these days but Joyce protects him. You know I think she's turning the kids against me."

"Come now Jonasi, why would she do that?"

"Joyce hates me. You know Essie I have done so much for Joyce and her kids and this is the thanks I get? Bloody bullshit. I'll just stop paying Tino's school fees and let's see what he'll do. At least Sarah baked me a cake. I thought Matipa would throw a big bash for me but she just looked at me and said where's the money Jonasi? I don't have the money. You know I do a lot for Matipa but she won't do anything for me. These days I'm lucky if I get fucked. Everything is about the twins. Sometimes I wonder if Joyce and Matipa would love me if I didn't have a cent."

"I'm sure they love you," I replied, stroking his thigh, straying to that bulge between his legs.

That put a huge smile on his face. If we were going to spend the afternoon together I did not want to hear him whining and whingeing about his other wives and kids. I did not get out often and those few times I did I wanted to make it count. So we arrived at Sam's Hideout. Jonasi's friend had created a pub in the middle of nowhere. The place was patronised by the usual suspects... overgrown men with adolescent kids on their arms. Now I could see why Jonasi was overly protective over Sarah. It was a jungle out there. I was probably the oldest woman there but trust me I held my own. Simon Chimbetu and the Four Brothers took the stage and entertained. We drank Castle Lager and I matched Jonasi bottle for bottle. We ate braaied offal, ox trotters, sausages and more *sadza*. I could match Jonasi bite for bite and did not care whether I had cellulite or tyres around my waist. I was extremely comfortable in my forty-something skin. Whatever I gained in weight I danced it off on the dusty dance floor. I shook my fleshy behind in a way that would put Beyoncé to shame. You see because of my kids I get to watch MTV against my will and trust me I could teach those girls a thing or two. I gyrated against Jonasi until I could feel his erection through my denim skirt. At one point he could not dance anymore and was just holding onto my waist watching my ass move on its own.

"Let's go home," he bellowed. "We need to finish this off at home."

We did not make it home. We had done about five

kilometres on the road and my bladder was about to burst.

"Jonasi stop the car. I'm pressed!"

"Essie where will you piss? We are in the middle of the bush."

"Jona stop the car!" I screamed.

He swerved onto the side of the road and came to a screeching halt. I climbed out of the car and he put the headlights on full beam.

"Piss where I can see you," he shouted.

So I went right in front of him and bunched my skirt around my waist. Then I bent down and pissed. All I could hear were crickets and hooting owls. I had no tissue to wipe so I just stood up and shook and all the time Jonasi was watching me. Then I bent over double and balanced my hands on the ground and really shook my ass like I was on MTV starring in some rap star's video. The beads around my waist clashed together. Jonasi turned off the ignition and got out of the car. He shagged me on the side of the road. He pumped me hard and fast like he was possessed by some demon. He growled and I howled. Primal instinct took over as we literally tore each other apart with a raging desire. This was the old Jonasi I knew, rough and rugged around the edges.

seventeen

I lay on my back, knees drawn up to my chest, suffering the humiliation at the hands of my gynae after being told I had contracted an STI. I'm dark so even if I blushed it wouldn't show but I burned with shame and embarrassment. My temperature must have probably shot through the roof. It all began about three weeks ago I had started getting this pasty brown discharge which had a rather offensive smell. I thought it was just a mild yeast infection and got something over the counter. However things did not get better, they only got worse. I remember one night I had sex with Jonasi and I had such violent cramps I almost keeled over in pain. Then I started to bleed. It was sporadic but I would bleed intermittently. That's when I called my gynae and decided to go in for a check-up. I was thinking it might be cervical cancer or something grand. Only to be told I had gonorrhoea.

"The symptoms usually go unnoticed in women," explained my gynae. "Your partner probably had the symptoms earlier."

If Jonasi had been aware of the STI, what had he done

about it and when was he going to put me in the loop?

"Look, I'm going to put you on a course of antibiotics" she continued. "And during this time I want you to refrain from sex. Your partner will have to come in for treatment."

"I'll let him know," I replied as I pulled up my lacy Triumph underwear.

"You know it would also be in your best interests to get an HIV test."

Now I felt like cymbals were crashing in my ears. My gynae read the fear in my eyes.

"I'm not saying you are positive but just as a precautionary measure. It's not all STIs that are HIV related."

"Fine," I replied.

She agreed to do the tests for me and told me to check for my results in the next couple of days. I drove home feeling dejected. Was Jonasi really worth it? At least if I had the assurance that Jonasi slept with Joyce and me only but I could not even say that with certainty. There were times when I could not find Jonasi and I would call Joyce and even she would not know where he was. It was obvious he was screwing around on the both of us. I had tried not to let it get to me. Told myself I was the big picture. Now that picture was stained with an STI. Since my "marriage" to Jonasi I had been faithful. Why would I want to be screwing around when I had everything I wanted under one roof? Jonasi was my one-stop shop for money, sex, power, conversation and entertainment. However the glaring reality was that neither Joyce nor I were enough for him. He was a greedy, selfish prick and we would never be able to satiate his desires. Gawd help him if I had Aids. I would kill him with my own hands. I was seething by the time I got home but the twins managed to cheer me up as they came running towards me, their poor nanny running after them. They were in the terrible-twos stage and ran amok around the house. I loved my girls and my heart constricted when I held them both. I could not afford to get sick and die. That would mean I would miss out on their first day of school. Miss out on their first Holy Communion. Miss out on their 21st birthdays. I would miss out on every other day of their lives in between and for what? Just because of an orgasm? (Come to think of it, I could not even remember the last time I had even come.) I know I love money and power but I love my daughters more. They were still young, so very young. If I died, who would take care of them? Jonasi might be able to provide for them financially but who would sustain them emotionally? No one in the world could love my girls the way I did. I bathed with them in my heart-shaped bathtub. It was our daily evening ritual. I would fill the bath with essential oils and lavender and my girls and I would be immersed inside. They loved the bubbles and they would splash water in my face and all over the floor. I did not care; I did not have to clean up. When I came out of the bathtub, Jonasi was standing in the doorway. The girls ran to him in delight. Jonasi was carrying them in his arms but his eyes were fixated on my naked body and my newly acquired gold belly ring. I actually wanted to cover myself from his leering eyes.

"Don't I get a kiss?" he asked

"No you don't," I replied flatly reaching for a white fluffy towel to wrap around my body.

He took off with the girls and when he returned I had slipped into a pink negligee. He looked extremely disappointed.

"I thought I would find you hot and naked?"

I cut him off glibly, "I'm not in the mood for sex."

"Matipa, what do I have to do to get sex around here? Have you and Joyce decided to go on a sex strike? How does it happen that I can't get sex from my own wives? Do I need to pay you to have sex, is that it?"

"Jonasi stop behaving like the twins. I'm not the only person you screw so don't try the wounded-dog act with me."

"Matipa what the hell is that supposed to mean?"

"Exactly that Jonasi. I went to the doctor today and he told me I have an STD. If you are going to sleep around Jonasi, at least wear a condom..."

I did not even finish what I wanted to say. Jonasi slapped me so hard across the face that I stumbled and fell back onto the bed. He removed the leather belt around his waist and beat me with it. I held up my hands to cover my face but I got a good strapping on my legs, my thighs and on my back. I bit down on my tongue down to hold back the screams. I think that enraged Jonasi even more because he lifted my nightie and whipped me with the metal part of the belt across my fleshy behind. I had no idea what imprint his assault left on me but the pain stung my entire body.

"Jonasi, no! No!" I screamed.

My anguished cries only spurred him on to hit me harder. He had developed a steady rhythm and I could almost anticipate the lashing from the belt every 10 seconds. I closed my eyes and lost count of the number of strokes he lashed out at me. I don't know how long it was before he stopped but eventually he did. At first I thought he was catching his breath until I felt him pull me to the edge of the bed. Jonasi spread my ass cheeks apart and forced himself into me. He thrust into me with wild abandon. He gripped me around my waist so I could not wriggle away. The pain was crippling. I shrieked out till my throat was dry and parched. He grabbed my hair roughly and made me look at him as he came inside me. There was no love in those eyes, just venom and malice. He finally withdrew his limp penis from inside me and pushed me onto the bed. I lay paralysed with a combination of pain and fear. I could feel the warm blood trickling in the crack of my ass. When he came out of the bathroom he started to get dressed. I could not even turn away because my neck hurt.

"Don't talk to me like I'm shit, Matipa. Learn to respect me; I'm your husband. *Muri mahure mese.* You are all whores. You think I don't know you love me for my money? I know. I can see through you, but I own you Matipa. I own you. You were bought and paid for, my dear, and if I want to screw you in the ears I will do just that."

After he had gone I literally crawled to the bathroom to clean myself up. I looked at myself in the mirror and cried all over again. My body was criss-crossed with welts. As I sat in a heap on the cold bathroom floor I felt nothing but unadulterated hatred for Jonasi.

I did not go to work the next day. My body ached from head to toe. I felt excruciating pain in places I never knew even existed. I could not even compare this to childbirth. At least with that when you held your baby in your arms you forgot. This pain stayed with me. Instead of taking two tablets as indicated on the box I took four. It was the only way I could be lulled to sleep. I had to take an overdose of painkillers so that I could get even a wink of sleep. Jonasi had flowers and chocolates delivered to the house. I told the maid to eat the chocolates and throw the flowers away. Even if Jonasi had sent me a diamond bracelet I would have thrown it away. No diamonds and pearls could have mollified me. I spent the rest of the week in bed, lying on my stomach. My bowels felt loose and each time I relived in my mind what had happened I would rush to the loo. Make no mistake about it, after that beating Jonasi gave me I was scared of him. Every night I got down on my knees and prayed he would not come round again and my prayers were answered. The weekend came with not even a whiff of Jonasi. I spent my Sunday stretched out on the patio on the wooden lounger soaking in the sun. The heat helped assuage my pain. The children were playing in the garden where I could see them. I had lathered them with SPF30. I did not care if I burned to a crisp. As dark as I was I could not get any darker. I drank my red wine, smoked and tried to read a book. I could not concentrate on either task. Joyce came round around 12 p.m. with Shumi. I figured they were coming from church. She was the last person I wanted to see, especially in the state I was in. My weave was uncombed; I had no make-up on and looked like a pathetic mess. She looked as good as always. Joyce is lucky, her beauty is effortless. She's like a pretty flower. She was wearing a flowing white dress and gold espadrilles. You wonder what more Jonasi could want in a woman.

"Hi Mattie," she called out. "I tried calling you on the cell but you were unreachable."

I was unreachable because I did not want to speak to anyone or see anyone, especially Joyce. My relationship with Joyce is superficial. I had no doubt in my mind that she hated me. Look I would be vain to expect anything else from her. I watched her as she crouched low to hug my daughters. Joyce lifted each one in turn into the air. I am sure she genuinely loved them because Joyce is a genuinely nice person. The sad thing is nice people don't get ahead in life. They have their corns stepped on. She came over to say hello. I forced myself to sit up. I was still sore and tender from Jonasi's brutal assault. I even winced in pain when she hugged me. She sat down in the armchair, crossing one leg over another. She was very elegant. I gasped in horror when she removed her Chanel sunglasses. She was nursing two black eyes. Here I was thinking I was in a bad state. If he could do that to her face I shuddered to think what her body was like.

"Joyce. What happened to you?"

"Jonasi happened," she replied.

You see Joyce is extremely light and now she had these dark patches around her like she was starring in the *Pirates of the Caribbean.*

"I guess it's been a bad week for everyone," I remarked drily.

"Why? What happened to you?"

I unbuttoned my loose fitting linen shirt. She held her hand to her mouth as she surveyed the marks all over my body. There was no doubt in her mind that I had been thoroughly beaten. I still had blotchy patches of red on my dark skin.

"Has he always been this abusive?" I asked.

"No," replied Joyce. "He had never hit me before but he came home on Wednesday night breathing fire. He said he wanted to have sex with me and I refused. That's when it all started..."

I could tell Joyce was about to cave in but she pulled herself and continued with the story.

"I told him to go to hell and then that's when he punched me across the face. You know Matipa, the beating was bad enough but then he raped me. He said I drove his cars, spent his money, the least I could do was open his legs to him. You know he did things to me that I can't even say. Things I can't even tell my own mother."

The tears were rolling down her face. She paused to wipe her face with a Kleenex. I was hoping she would tell me what he had done to her but she would not divulge a thing to me. Joyce was a lady like that.

"Joyce," I began, "You need to protect yourself. I'm being treated for an STD."

Joyce broke down and cried then. I reached out and hugged her. I had no words but I knew my touch communicated a thousand things to her. I think that's all she needed right then. I can take a lot of things but one thing I was not going to take was abuse in any form. I had come into this thing with Jonasi on my terms and those terms had not included physical abuse. I knew if I stayed with Jonasi I would end up like Joyce, my mother, my sister and all those other women who took abuse in all shapes and sizes. They had been reduced to blithering idiots. I felt like I was getting a preview into my future if I remained in Jonasi's life. I made up my mind then that I was going to walk away from all of this whilst I still had the chance.

eighteen

I was actually pained when Matipa left. It felt like someone in the family had died. I never expected her to just up and leave. None of us did actually. She came to drop off the twins one Saturday afternoon and just never returned to pick them up. I had gone to drop them off on a Sunday evening only to have the maid meet me at the door with a letter. No actually it would be wrong to call it that, it was just a note.

Dear Joyce
After what happened with Jonasi I am not sure I can just pick up from where we left off. Watch my girls for me. I know they are in safe hands.
Matipa

I know you are thinking I found her hanging from a chandelier with a sheet wrapped around her broken neck. I didn't. And neither did I find her sitting naked in the bath tub, with cut wrists, immersed in her own blood. Matipa had not committed suicide. She had just disappeared. She left her Mercedes Benz and Jeep parked in the garage. The house had been left in a spick-and-span condition, everything in place. She had only taken a few of her clothes and some jewellery. That alone gave us (Jonasi included), the impression that she had gone away for a few weeks. He said it was typical of Matipa to take "time out" when things got a little bit rough. He was confident she would be back after three weeks. A month passed. A month turned to two. That was when Jonasi confronted Matipa's mother demanding to know her whereabouts.

"You're the husband, you should know," replied Mrs Chando flippantly.

"Well I don't know," replied Jonasi. "That's why I'm asking."

"Well I don't know either," replied Mrs Chando. "We haven't heard from her."

Jonasi got really worried. He hired a private investigator to try and suss out her whereabouts. All he could tell us was that Matipa had caught a flight to Johannesburg on the evening of the 15th of July. The P.I. suspected she might have caught a connecting flight but no one knew where to. Jonasi fired him on the spot. That was not the kind of feedback he wanted to hear. However he could not tell you himself where Matipa was.

"Matipa's trying to get back at me," spoke Jonasi. "She'll be back when she's run out of money."

Like he had any money to hand out. Things were tight with us financially. We had survived the financial crisis of 2003 when many fly-by-night financial institutions like ENG Asset Management had met their early demise. If anything, 2003 was the year when Jonasi made a lot of his money. Now we were just coasting by. The economy had gone into decline and the operating environment was just difficult. We could not even afford to take a holiday abroad. The best Jonasi could do for us was Cape Town. Lucky Matipa wherever she was.

Six months elapsed and still no word from Matipa. Jonasi's worry turned to depression. He woke me up in the middle of the night.

"What if she's dead, Joyce?"

"She's not dead," I replied with conviction.

I knew she was alive because she had called one afternoon and asked to speak to the girls. She said she could not stay on the phone for long but she just wanted to hear their voices. She sounded distraught and tearful on the other end.

"Come home Matipa," I pleaded.

"I can't Joyce. Please take care of my babies."

She had hung up on me and that was the last I heard from Matipa. For a long time I was bitter that she had gone. You know we had become such good friends overnight. I had finally found someone I could confide in in a way I could not with my mother or my sisters. I felt betrayed that she would just up and leave me to fight the battle alone. I really felt let down. She had bailed out when she should have been here all the time giving me moral support. Now I was stuck with Jonasi. I know I should have been happy to have my husband back (and trust me he was back in full force) but for many reasons, I still felt resentful towards him.

"Joyce, does she call you?" he asked.

"No Jonasi. She doesn't call me."

"You know I should never have hit her. I should never have hit you both that day. I am really sorry Joyce. You don't know how sorry I am. Please don't leave me."

I exhaled deeply, "I won't."

Trust me if I had somewhere to dump my kids and vanish into oblivion I would have done the same as Matipa. Some of us just did not have the luxury. And some of us were not that selfish.

"Joyce, I love you and I know I have made mistakes but I want to make it up to you."

"Jonasi, let's just get some sleep," I replied turning away from him and giving him my back. I felt his hands come round my waist and he gripped me tightly. He curled into me and buried his face into my back. He cried then. Loud gut-wrenching sobs and I felt his entire body quake. Yes he might have been vulnerable but I was just fed up. How many nights had I cried alone with no one to hold my hand? I was tired of picking up the pieces and rebuilding the blocks of our marriage. Now I had inherited two daughters and God knows what else.

I could not find it in me to hate the twins. Sometimes I resented their presence. On those days I could even wallop their little bottoms for the silliest of things but afterwards they would cry and cling to me. Children have such a forgiving nature and pure innocent untainted hearts. How could you not love them? They reminded me I was human. My mother thought I was crazy and made sure to remind me at every opportunity.

"They are not your responsibility Joyce. Take them to Matipa's mother."

"She left them here. She left them with me."

"And where is Matipa? Screwing her head off somewhere? Joyce when will you stop being abused? So now you are Mother Zimbabwe? Why don't you just collect all of Jonasi's bastard kids?"

"Mum they are just kids!"

I won't lie to you, they were a handful. Ashley was the louder and more voracious of the two. Hayley just followed her lead. I took their nanny on to look after them. Look, I've had my fill of changing diapers and they were at that troublesome age where they needed to be watched 24/7. I just did not have the time or the energy. I also had Jonasi to contend with now. Save for Wednesday and Saturday, the days he played golf, Jonasi was always home. He even worked a lot more from home now and travelled less. If he was not in the study, he was watching television with Shumi and the twins. There were days I wished he could just disappear somewhere because he was starting to piss me off. I now had to cook lunch and supper for him. Sometimes I just bought takeaways and if he complained I would tell him I had to study. That was my excuse for everything. Jonasi could not wait until I finished my exams. I'd wait till then to break the news about varsity. I would have loved to go away for four years and leave Jonasi to take care of the house and the family. However that was a distant dream. The best I could do would be to start my articles. Come what may I knew I had a place at Stan's firm. We still talked but we had not gone out to dinner again since that time. We had almost crossed a line that night that we both knew we should not have. I was still very married to Jonasi. I rolled the rings around my fingers. They were like a noose now. Jonasi might have been home more often, trying hard to be the kind of husband I have always wanted him to be but I did not trust him one inch. Even when he stayed out late at night I always had the lurking suspicion he was with some other woman. He tried to reassure me he was faithful. I did not believe him. I had been evicted from that Fool's Paradise. That's why we used condoms now.

No, I used condoms. Look, I knew I was never going to get Jonasi to wear one so I did. You must be wondering how I got away with this one without being beaten. Well I just told him after the STD fiasco that the doctor said I should use them until I was clear. I got the doctor to lie on my behalf that the symptoms took longer to clear in women. He bought it. That was why six months later we were still on rubber and it was going to stay that way. The phone rang, breaking through into my thoughts. Now that Jonasi worked from home, his PA diverted all his calls to the house. You have no idea how much that pissed me off because I now had to double up as the receptionist. It was bad enough I had to do other things for Jonasi.

"Hello," I said not masking the annoyance in my voice.

"Hello. Could I speak to Mr Gomora?"

"He's out," I replied staunchly.

"When will he be home?"

"I don't know," I replied, "Midnight maybe. Was there anything urgent?"

"Yes," came the reply. "Please could you tell him that Mum is critical? They are not sure if she'll make it through the night."

"Who's your mum?" I asked.

"Essie," she replied.

"Essie from where?"

"Warren Park."

"Oh okay," I replied.

Now it made sense. *Tete* Essie. I had not seen her in ages. Almost two years to be exact. I don't know how she was related to Jonasi. I think she was a sister from another mother or his dad's brother's daughter or whatever. Anyway I tried to avoid my husbands' relatives wherever possible. They were loud mouthed and undignified. They always had mad drama going on. I think it was Wonder who literally stank up the place at my husband's 40th. How do you get so drunk as to shit on yourself? Essie was worse. She got so drunk and starting dancing *kwasa kwasa*. You know that typical growth-point behaviour.

"Where is she?" I asked.

"Parirenyatwa Hospital," she replied.

That was not too bad. I could drive out there without any problems. I looked at my gold Cartier watch. I would be able to make it in good time for the 4 p.m.-visiting hour. I asked Essie's daughter to meet me at the parking lot because I did not want to spend hours looking for them. I recognised her immediately. She had an uncanny resemblance to Jonasi. She could have been his younger sister from the same mother. I waved to her in acknowledgement. She came forward then and threw her arms around me. I stood stiff in her embrace. I did not think that was really necessary.

"Thank you for coming," she gushed, "I really appreciate this."

I could not exactly tell her I had no choice could I? I smiled instead and followed her into the hospital. I was greeted by the smell of death intermingled with excreta and antiseptic. I held my hand to my nose.

"I know it's awful, but after a while you forget the smell."

For the first time I realised she spoke very good English and was pretty well mannered for a township girl. The fruit had really fallen far from the tree. Walking into Essie's room I was not surprised to find the usual suspects: Wonder and his wife, Gershom with his. They all came forward to greet me with reverence. That's the sad thing about money, kudos is given where it is not deserved. Jonasi was the youngest brother but they treated him like he was the head of the family because he had the most money. Nothing was done without Jonasi's approval. I remember one time they postponed a burial because Jonasi was away in Belgium.

"MaiGuru," said Gershom holding onto my hand longer than necessary, "it was good of you to come."

You have no idea how much I hated that name. It added twenty years to me. I walked over to the bed to peer at Essie. I could not even make out her form in the blankets. The Essie I know is fat. The woman lying in that cot was a thinned-down version of Essie. She looked like she had been baked in an oven and left there for too long. Essie was a pretty woman. Then again which fat woman have you ever seen who's not pretty?

"Essie," I called out, "can you hear me?"

She did not respond.

"The doctor won't say what it is," said Wonder coming forward, "But whatever it is, it's bad."

Trust me it was bad. I could not deal with this. Jonasi had to come over and take control of things. Just as Sarah had said, I was not sure if *Tete* Essie would make it through the night.

nineteen

I survived. I am a survivor but I won't lie, the battle had ravaged me. I looked at myself in the mirror and shuddered because I could not recognise that gaunt woman staring back at me. The hair on the sides of my head had been eroded by my pillows. I had been bedridden for months. I could not believe I was finally going home. You don't really value life until you have been gripped in the jaws of death. Sarah ran a brush through the straggly strands of hair that remained on my head. I had a good mind to shave my head when I got home. My skin was sallow and all the shine I ever had was gone. I had aged so much. I looked like I was my mother's older sister. I don't know how many kilograms I had lost but I was now thinner than Sarah. The slip hung on my skeletal frame. Even my breasts looked like dried prunes. I turned away from the mirror. I could not bear to look at this woman anymore.

"You are looking well Mama," commented Sarah.

I did not believe her. She was probably saying that just to make me feel better. That was what they all said. People lie to you. They say you look great when you actually look and smell like something that has been dragged out of a rubbish heap. I was never short of visitors. Wonder, Gershom and their wives had been regulars, constant companions who tried to make me laugh even when it looked like all hope had been lost. Jonasi had come too. My poor darling, he had been deeply affected by my sickness, but I was okay now. One person I had not expected to come by was Joyce, enveloped in a cloud of perfume that almost made me choke. She had come many times and sat at my bedside muttering obscenities. She thought I could not hear her but I heard everything she said to me. She behaved like the queen but you would be shocked by the trash that came out of her mouth. Anyway when I get my strength back I am going to sort her out. I will beat the living daylights out of her. She thinks she's God's gift to the world. I will set her straight and show her the light. The other person who had strayed to my bedside and who I would much rather not have seen was Freedom. I could not believe he had taken time off from his life of crime and grime to come and perch at my bedside. Then I knew why he had come. Trust me he was not motivated by sympathy, rather by greed. He just wanted to make sure I had a first-class ticket to hell. I know for a fact that I was not hallucinating when he grabbed me by the neck and asked me where I had hidden my bank cards. If there was anyone who knew anything about my finances, it was Sarah. She was the only one I could trust. Everyone else was just waiting for me to die so they could take over what I had. My mother had moved into my house. My sisters had started helping themselves to my clothes, my shoes, my linen and my dinner sets. Sarah told me Freedom was already rolling round the hood in my BMW.

I knew I would be in for more surprises when I got home.

"I'll take you for a manicure and a pedicure," continued Sarah. "I'll have you looking brand new like Auntie Joyce."

My daughter was secretly enamoured with Joyce. She had always known her father had another wife but I think in her head she thought Joyce was another me. I think Joyce far exceeded her expectations with her beauty and class. But you know what; her tonnes of class could not keep Jonasi from the likes of us. A pussy was a pussy. They did not have "class" written on them. Even my dirty, smelly pussy could top hers any day.

"I don't want to look like Joyce," I replied. "I just want to look like me."

Right now I looked like I had woken up from the dead. That someone had gone to Mbudzi cemetery and dug me out and tipped me out of the coffin and blown life back into me. It's been a rough road to recovery. But I was determined to live. I grabbed life by the balls and said I was going to exist by hook or by crook. I had fought the battle and won. The doctors said I had TB but I knew that was not true. Joyce had done something to me. I had been full of life until the last winter when I got a bout of the flu that just would not go away. Then I started coughing. First I took Woods for it but when I started coughing blood I knew there was more to it. I decided to go and visit Philemon in Dzivarasekwa. He was a faith healer and had helped me a lot in the past.

Philemon lived in a two-roomed house that was on its last legs. Although it was not signposted, you knew you were in the right place because there was a long queue of people outside seeking help too. This was the new Zimbabwe: queues for bread, queues for sugar and even longer queues to see a faith healer. And in the new Zimbabwe, money spoke volumes and I had a lot of it. I made my way past the tiny gate, which was barely held together by the loose hinges. Philemon, dressed in a sweeping white robe, rushed forward to meet me. He greeted me respectfully. I accorded him the same respect. He led me into the house, weaving past the queues of people who sat in the scorching sun. Before I entered the house I had to remove my shoes. The house was dark with a glimmer of light coming in from the open door. The acrid smell of poverty crept up and into my nostrils. I settled down on a decrepit sofa, which was hollow inside and threatened to swallow my whole backside. A wispy curtain separated the lounge from the bedroom. The groans of an ailing man would intermittently interrupt the proceedings on the other side. A younger woman was cooking on the two-plate stove, oblivious to what was going on around her. I clapped my hands together; greeting the faith healer who sat on the threadbare carpet, which like everything else in the room needed a facelift. MaiTino, as she was called, was from the Vapostori sect. She had healing powers and helped many people with problems ranging from asthma to infertility to lack of sexual prowess. I had learned about MaiTino many years ago from our neighbour. She had seen the picture of Jonasi and Joyce in the local paper following their lavish wedding. It had been one of those weddings where the "who's who" of Harare had attended. Even the president had been there. She had called me over and pointed at the picture.

"My child, you lost out on this?"

I nodded quietly.

"This could have all been all yours. I used to watch that boy. He was in love with you. How did it slip from within your grasp?"

I shrugged. I knew why. Well at least I thought I knew why until that woman pointed something out to me that I had never ever considered before.

"You were stupid Essie. You should have consulted your ancestors. How do you think some women end up walking down the aisle in white? They consult."

I was puzzled. I had no idea what she meant. She could see I was clueless. She laughed at my naivety.

"Essie did you never stop to ask yourself why you have been plagued with bad luck? A man who promised to marry you gets killed in the war. Then Jonasi who loved you leaves you to marry another woman. Something is very wrong Essie. You need to consult. This is what this Joyce girl did. Now look at her, smiling from ear to ear. She is walking around with that gold on her finger. It doesn't matter how many kids you have with him Essie, the fact is that he is now married to someone else. The best you can do is become his second wife. I know a woman who can help you."

So I had approached MaiTino and I have never looked back since. She helped me get betrothed. At one point I had almost given up on anything happening but she made the breakthrough. She ensured that Jonasi always gave me money. That is why even when Jonasi and I were having problems he never stopped giving me money. That is why he still supported my children and made sure they were well provided for. I knew many other "wives" who had been left out in the cold. Who had to fight to get two cents. I had never had such problems. Women come and go from Jonasi's life but I was still here. I would never forget MaiTino and I rewarded her generously.

"Are you well my child?" spoke maiTino, "You don't look well."

I coughed then and some phlegm landed on my lap.

"I'm not well. I can't even sleep at night."

The woman nodded sagely, "You come with a bad aura. I sensed it long before you walked in. I was filled with heaviness. I knew you were on your way."

"What is it?" I asked, holding a hand to my chest. "What do you see?"

The woman's eyes widened. Her pupils were dark like coals. She started to shake her head vehemently.

"MaiFreedom you are going to die if you are not careful..."

As she spoke, the woman seemed to veer off into another realm, far removed from where we were and then, just as quickly as she had gone, she was quickly brought back.

"Is it Joyce?" I asked in desperation. "Is she trying to kill me?"

The woman shook her head vehemently, "This is bigger than Joyce. I am going to give you some water. I want you to sprinkle some of it in your house and the remaining liquid you must use to bath. And as you bath I want you to call out to your ancestors."

I took MaiTino's advice like it was the gospel. She had never let me down before so why would she start now? Her able assistant brought in a two-litre container of water and then both of them bowed their heads and began to pray feverishly. They prayed in a language that I could not understand. I got a little nervous when MaiTino's voice changed into a high-pitched crescendo. She looked like she was possessed by some other spiritual being. When calm and sanity prevailed over them once again, MaiTino handed me the bottle of water. In turn I thanked them with sheets of money. They both showed their appreciation by clapping their hands together. I left then, passing the long, winding queue outside. It was for this reason that I had faith in this woman. Why would all these people be here if she did not provide answers to their problems?

So much for having faith in MaiTino, instead of getting better I got worse. The coughing got worse, especially in the mornings. I lost my appetite and you know how I love to eat, but I just had no desire for anything. Often I had bad dreams and would wake up in a cold sweat, my sheets soaking wet. I would have to change my bed linen and my nightie. I wanted to go and see MaiTino again but I was weak and tired. When Sarah came home for the holidays she took one look at me and drove me to the doctor. I tried to resist her but I was too weak. All the while I tried to tell her there was nothing the doctor could do for me, that my condition was not medical but rather someone out there was trying to fix me. At least now I knew who my enemies were and I was going to watch my back. Joyce had better watch out too because I was coming for her.

twenty

Just as I thought my luck was running out, providence shone down on me. You see it had been over a year since I had moved in with Farai and I was even further from getting what I wanted. In all that time I'd had three abortions and now I was on my seventh pregnancy and I told Farai I was keeping it. He just looked at me like I was out of my mind.

"If you keep it, you'll raise the bastard on your own!"

"How can you say that about your own child?"

"It's not a child. Just abort and save us both the hassle. You are the one who's stupid enough to get pregnant. Why don't you use contraception or something?"

"I'm not going to abort," I replied stubbornly.

"Don't think you can trap me into marrying you by falling pregnant. I'm going to be a father when I'm goddamn ready."

Farai had never been hesitant about sticking it inside me and getting me pregnant. Now he was reading me the riot act on how to avoid pregnancies. Deep down I had been secretly hoping he would get tired of forking out money for abortions and be excited about the thought of us having a baby together. That he would actually make things official and marry me. However, the graffiti was on the wall. He did not want me or his babies. I figured at this rate, I could have aborted myself and he would not have cared. You see he would not give me a dime but come abortion time and he would splurge. And abortions were not getting any cheaper. The few doctors who performed them were scared of getting their licences revoked for the illegal procedures so you had to pay through the nose. I really did not want to have another abortion. I realised I had a conscience and it was starting to kick in. What would it hurt if I kept this baby? Most babies grew up with less. Then I thought of giving my baby the life I'd had and that made me shudder. Even if I wanted to step out on my own I did not have the money to support myself. Although I continued to service Tito, Rhino and Jonasi on the side, it was not as frequent as I would have liked. Even the money was not that great anymore. I guess everyone was feeling the pinch of the economic woes of Zimbabwe. No one was immune, even Jonasi. Gone were the willy-nilly deposits into my account. I flipped through the newspaper looking through the 'Flats to rent' column. The rentals being asked for were astronomical. Some were quoted in US-dollar terms. I sighed in despair. There was no way I could afford that on my meagre salary. I was lucky to have a job still. Nowadays people were being retrenched left, right and centre. I guess the reason they still had me at the reception was because it did not cost the company much to keep me there. Still those peanuts helped me get by. I needed them now more than ever. I suppose the other option would have been to share with someone. I dreaded the thought of sharing with a girlfriend. Next thing they would be in on your business and before you knew it they would be in on your men. I stirred my cold cup of coffee. Right at that moment I yearned for a full English breakfast from Wimpy. I could almost smell the freshly ground coffee and crispy fried bacon and sunrise eggs that were soft and runny in the middle. I could vividly visualise the freshly baked scones filled with gooseberry jam and dollops of thick cream. The more I fantasised about them the more unbearable my craving became. I could not even afford to buy a queen cake from Baker's Inn. The spirit of brokenness was upon me. So was the spirit of discord and disunity. Farai did not pick me up from work that evening so I had to beg a lift off one of the girls in the office. I did not have enough money to catch a cab and could not contemplate going home any other way. I would not, and I repeat I would not, be caught dead climbing into an emergency taxi. I would probably break my heels walking to the rank. Not to mention the humiliation of being spotted flagging down cars. I might have been down but I was not out. I had a reputation to maintain as one of the It Girls of Harare. Even if things were not good I had to keep up the façade.

Farai came home after midnight. I had been counting the hours. He was behaving like such a bastard these days. We fought every night and he had gone off my pussy like it was sour cream. Even my looks did not move him. If anything my presence repulsed him. I figured whoever he was seeing on the side was driving him crazy. Men get all cocky like that when they are having some hot action on the side. Before, things like this never bothered me because I knew with time they inevitably burned out. Now I knew otherwise, it was only a matter of time before Farai threw me out of his apartment if I did not move out of my own accord. Farai had had enough of me. When you strip naked in front of someone and they don't even twitch you know your time is up. Even that night I pressed my titties into his back to try and elicit some sort of reaction and he moved away from me. So I lay on my back, staring at the ceiling, plotting my next move.

"Farai. Could I have abortion money?"

I asked like I was asking for money for bread and milk.

"How much do you need?"

I called out a crazy amount. Although it was dark I could visualise him frowning with disgust.

"That much?"

"Yes," I replied, "Inflation."

Hyperinflation, not even inflation had contributed to the demise of the Zimbabwean economy. It was rampant, rife and totally uncontrollable. We now dealt with millions and very soon it would be trillions.

"Okay. I'll transfer the money to your account."

I turned to my side and slept. I had sweet dreams that night. I was not going to use that money for an abortion. I was going to use it to put a deposit on a flat I had identified in the paper. I would figure out a way to pay the rent money. That afternoon I got a call from Jonasi. He wanted to see me after work. He said he had booked a room at the Oasis and that he would send his driver to pick me up after work. You see what I mean; things were tough. Before the only places Jonasi and I slept in were the Crown Plaza and the Meikles. Now we had to trade down to 3-star hotels in the Avenues. Anyway it did not bother me. I had shagged men in worse places. I really pulled out the fireworks and left him slumped and exhausted. There was nothing I would not and could not do. Jonasi was a kinky man behind those tailored suits. He was sexually adventurous and would go places others would not dare to explore. He also got off on role play and hardcore porn flicks. At times he wanted me to masturbate in front of him. I obliged his every fantasy. Like I said before, there was nothing I would not do, especially where he was involved. Afterwards as he lay in my arms like a satiated, contented cat I knew I could ask for money and I would not be denied.

"What do you need all that money for?" he asked.

"I've been evicted from my flat," I replied with a sulky pout. "I have nowhere to go."

He looked at me with obvious concern, "Well I have an empty house you can stay in. Besides it will save us spending so much money on hotel bills. That way I can also screw you whenever I want to."

I threw my arms around him and showered him with kisses.

"Thank you my darling. Thank you!"

So the very next day I moved into Jonasi's house in Ballantyne Park. I did not want to give him time to change his mind. Not that he would, Jonasi is a man of his word. He sent the driver to drop off the keys at my workplace. Farai called me that evening to say he was not coming home and that I should not leave any supper for him. I did not flip. I now had my Plan "A" in place. I did not need Farai and his sick abuse. I was moving onto bigger and better things and trust me the Ballanytne home was beautiful beyond any expectation I had. It was the kind of home you saw in magazines like *Garden and Home.* Even in my wildest dreams I had never envisioned myself ensconced in such luxury. It was tastefully furnished and all I had to do was walk in with my suitcase and hang things in the closet and put my folded clothes in the drawers. I also had a housekeeper which helped because there was no way I would have managed to keep such a big place neat and tidy. To top it all, Jonasi gave me the keys to a Mercedes that was parked in the garage. In a matter of seconds I had gone from zero to hero! I jumped on the bed with untold excitement. My baby was going to have a better life than I ever imagined possible. The only thing that put a dent on my good mood was when Farai called.

"You forgot your toiletries in the bathroom," he said.

"You can throw them away," I replied with insouciance.

"Fine."

Then he hung up. There was none of that: "Baby come home I miss you" or "Baby how you could leave me without saying goodbye?" I guess when he had come home and found my stuff gone he had said "good riddance". Still, that hurt. Look we had spent two years together. Surely that should have counted for something? Whoever said love hurt was dead right. It hurt like a motherfucker. Well I was going to make him sorry for ever treating me badly.

The abortion money came through to my account and I used it to buy a driver's licence. With the change I bought perfume and killer heels. I made sure to drive by Farai's building every evening until one evening he saw me entrenched inside the Mercedes with pure leather seats. I made sure to pull up to him, pull down the window and greet him gaily. He did a double take. He literally went green with envy.

"And this?" he asked, failing to swallow the lump that had developed in his throat.

"I'm now with a man who knows how to treat a woman," I replied.

I drove off then. Served him right for thinking he was the King Bee for driving an Isuzu Twin Cab. Well I was now the Queen Bitch driving a Mercedes. If he thought he had seen the last of me, he had another thing coming. The next time he saw me I was hanging on Jonasi's arms at a banking conference in Nyanga. I looked good, damn good. I wore a tight gold-sequinned number that had a lethally low back, so low that you could see the crack of my ass and the gold belly chain around my waist. The dress had a plunging neckline. One silly move and my breasts would be out in the open. My pregnancy had inflated them and they were growing bigger every day. I was four months along now and anyone with a wise eye could see the bulging tummy. But nonetheless, that did not decrease my sex appeal. I was the young hot thing on Jonasi's arms and every man in that room was drooling all over my golden body. Men were literally tripping over themselves to get a word or two to me when Jonasi was not looking. Each time I moved, the dress would move too. It had long slits that exposed my smooth long bronze legs. Jonasi held onto me for dear life. You have no idea how much I boosted his profile. He was the envy of every man in the business world. They wanted a piece of my ass but my ass now had Jonasi tattooed across it. The only time I left Jonasi's side was to go to the bathroom. When I came out of the ladies I was accosted by Farai.

"Peeps said you get around but I had no idea it was this far? If there's a trophy for bitching you deserve it. You're a slut."

"Don't call me a slut," I replied

"What should I call you?" he replied.

"I have a name and my name will do just fine."

I was about to swing away when he grabbed me by the

hand. I shrugged him off with all the force I could muster then I dusted my hand lightly like it had been tainted by his touch.

"Don't touch what you can't afford!" I hissed.

He laughed, "Trust me, I've been there and done that."

That hurt. Even though I walked off with all the dignity I could muster, swinging my mushrooming ass from side to side I bore the full brunt of his scathing words. I found refuge in the arms of Jonasi. He could tell I was hot and flustered. You see that's the thing about love. You love someone too much and they always have the power to hurt you in some way.

"What's wrong pumpkin?"

"That man," I said pointing out in Farai's direction "was coming on to me."

I could see Jonasi clench his fists and his forehead creased with untold anxiety. You see Jonasi is extremely possessive. More so now that I told him I am pregnant with his child. I had burst out the news one night after he had come into my mouth. He had not even doubted paternity. He had embraced it like it was his own. Look a little white lie never hurt anybody. What were the chances of him ever finding out the baby was not his? I had to play my cards right. Or as my mother would say,

"Don't waste the fanny my dear, let it work for you."

And trust me it was working wonders.

Farai got retrenched from work. He was given a generous package. Its karma, what goes around comes around. He called me frothing and fuming around the ears.

"Did you get me fired?"

"Why would I do that?" I replied innocently.

"To spite me? You are a vicious whore!"

"You still want to call me names? Do that again and I'll

make sure you never work in Harare ever again."

I cut the phone and felt immense satisfaction. I was lying outstretched on a chaise longue by the pool, wearing a bright red bikini, eating strawberries. My tummy was now spilling out onto my lap. I was six months along now. I was swollen and shiny like an overripe tomato. I had caught the gardener leering at me a couple of times. I had even opened my legs wider for him. Just teasing him a little. He had a tight ass and strong arms. I was so horny nowadays I was tempted to shag him. However I could not risk everything I had now for a few minutes of mind-blowing sex. Jonasi had really set me up. I no longer had to work. Jonasi insisted I take it easy and rest. If I had known having a baby with Jonasi would have gotten me this far I would have done it a long time ago. So I played the role of a pampered mistress who lives in a mansion. The housekeeper, Grace, became a good friend of mine. When she was done with the housework she would come and sit by me and keep me company. Grace would keep me entertained with stories about Matipa. Apparently she had been a bat out of hell and Grace said she had been elated when she left.

"Why did she leave?" I asked

"She had a big fight with Sir. I could not hear what they were fighting about but he beat her up. She was foul mouthed and had an attitude. After everything Sir did for her she was not grateful. She deserved to go. I hope you don't go. I like you Lindani."

Grace had nothing to worry about. I was not going anywhere. My feet were now stuck in a pot of honey and they would have to amputate them to get me out.

twenty-one

Jonasi did not live to walk Rudo down the aisle. I know it sounds mean but it's a good thing he died when he did. I don't know how Rudo felt but I sure as hell did not want a half-baked corpse hanging on my arm. That's what Jonasi looked like in the end. You know there are some things you can't say to people but between you and me he was a rotten, smelly carcass in the end. You know the day he died I felt relief; pure and utter relief. It's like a painful chapter of my life had come to an end. I suppose if Jonasi had accepted that he was HIV positive he might have been alive today. He might still have been whoring like there was no tomorrow. Some men just think monogamy is a wood that grows in the Eastern Highlands. They don't realise the virtues of being faithful and true to your loved ones. You see Jonasi had been breeding the virus under his own nose. I reckon he got it from Essie. That woman was filthy inside out. Oh I found out that *Tete* Essie was actually Jonasi's mistress. Then again you probably knew that. Why is it that the wife is always the last to know? Surely I should have been the first to know? How I found out was really innocent, quite ironic actually. Remember that time when Essie was close to death and everyone was about to read her last rites and her daughter called me to see her? Jonasi also popped round to see her that night. So whilst we were getting ready for bed he turns and says to me: "Essie is really in bad shape."

"I know. I don't think she'll make it through the night," I replied.

"If she dies can we take her kids in?"

I did a double take and my jaw nearly dropped to the ground. Why in the hell would we take Essie's kids in? Surely Essie had her sisters and brothers and God knows which other extended family who could open their home to them. Why did we always have to bear the brunt of other people's burdens?

"Why Jonasi? Don't they have a father?"

"I'm their father Joyce. When I said I had two other kids I meant Sarah and Blessing. Look you have taken the twins in. Why can't you take them too?"

Needless to say, that night Jonasi slept in the guest room after I had literally thrashed him with my fists. All these years I had looked at Essie and thought she was some close relative yet she was having the last laugh shagging Jonasi to high kingdom come. They had two grown kids – not one, but two! And the way Gershom and Wonder were so cosy with her made me realise they had always known. Once again everyone was having the last laugh at my expense. I cried that night. I cried so hard that my ribs hurt. I woke up early just in time for the 6 a.m. visit. Essie was alive, I'm sure she wished she were dead because I told her exactly where to shove it. As ailing as she was I grabbed her by the neck and thrashed her frail head against the pillow. I could have killed

Essie if the nurses had not restrained me but you don't understand the enormity of the anger inside of me. You see at least Matipa came out into the open with her fangs and made it clear to me who she was and what she was about. However little Essie pretended to be family yet she was screwing my husband left, right and centre. The realisation that Essie had always been there, lurking in the background hurt me more than I could ever imagine. I thought of the number of occasions I had seen her fat ass. At family weddings, family funerals, birthdays, you name it, she was there. What broke my heart even more was that Essie had not been just a fleeting affair; our existence had been parallel, deliberate and purposeful. It made a complete mockery of my marriage. To think I almost had a nervous breakdown because of Matipa yet there were more lethal weapons out there. I could not even begin to fathom the attraction between Jonasi and Essie. When I looked at Essie I only saw a fat uncultured lump of lard. Okay so she was a pretty fat uncultured lump of lard but what had been the attraction between them? Jonasi always moaned when I got fat so what was the deal with Essie? I was afraid to ask him even because somehow I knew deep down the answer would humiliate me and I had already been humiliated enough. I tell you Essie was the last straw. She was the nail in the coffin and from then onwards. I felt nothing but deep abhorrence for the man. You can't mask that kind of hate. He felt it alright because it was coming out of my pores and any other crevice in my body. He remained in the guest room permanently and never made any attempt to move back to our bedroom because I was literally spitting fire. When he could no longer stomach my attitude he moved out.

"I'm going to live with my new wife. Don't think because

you don't want me other women out there don't."

"They can have you Jonasi," I replied acidly, " Every rotten piece of you."

I was not hurt. I don't think after what Jonasi put me through I was capable of feeling any more pain. A burning abhorrence for Jonasi consumed me. I was glad to see him go. He could have died there for all I cared. And do you know what, he almost did.

We had been estranged for almost two years when word reached me that Jonasi was extremely sick. By then we only saw each other when it was absolutely necessary. I remember he showed up for Rudo's 21st birthday. We had decided to have a small braai at home with family and a few friends. When I say small, it was really small. The noughties were extremely rough. I could no longer splurge like I had in the past. Sometimes I would wake up and think the life I had lived previously had been all but a dream. Reality bites and Jonasi had tightened the purse strings. I don't even think tightened was the right word. To put it crudely, he would not give me a cent. He said I did not deserve any of his hard-earned cash since I was no longer fucking him. That's what you get after 19 years of marriage. It made me wish I had divorced Jonasi when I had the chance. At least then I might have walked away with the house and alimony. The only good thing was that both Rudo and I worked now so we could keep things going on the home front because I tell you Jonasi did not even give us money for groceries or the general upkeep. The gardener stayed on only because he had nowhere to go. He only worked three times a week and pimped himself to anyone else who needed gardening services. I kept his wife as our maid and she was there to clean up after the twins and Garikai. After my son had failed his "O" Levels, he decided he would just sit around the house and watch DSTV because he thought the world and Jonasi owed him something. Like Jonasi gave a damn. Even the twins who were once his pride and joy had been moved to a government school. They now hobnobbed with all the other gardeners' kids in the area and had the accents to show for it. Jonasi did not care; he said that's where they belonged. Matipa was still missing in action, so her input into their lives, financial or otherwise was zero. Look, I did the best I could under the circumstances. I dressed them in Power Sales clothing, just as long as they did not walk around naked. I won't even talk about myself. I can't even remember the last time I went shopping. The good thing is that I had always bought quality designer clothing and they did stand the test of time and I still looked very classy and elegant. My sisters also sent me clothing so my ass was still covered in that regard. Tino had started working in England after finishing his degree. He had no intention of ever coming back to Zimbabwe to work. I did not blame him; we had been to hell and back and things were only just starting to look up. Tino did send me money every now and then. At least I was able to get my car serviced because on my salary I could not afford it. I was working for one of the Big Four now and I was battling with my FQE exams. I tell you I wanted to qualify more than ever. My mentor, Stanslous, had since left the country and was now based in South Africa. We were still in touch. He would call me a lot and I was sure to drop him an email every now and then. Each time he came down he would bring me a bottle of expensive perfume and always take me out to lunch: things I previously took for granted when I thought the money tree was rooted in my backyard. J&J Holdings was no more. The company had been delisted from several bourses a few years back, been unbundled and sold off in bits and pieces. The bank had been closed down due to capitalisation problems. The microfinance arm had been sold to another bank. The stock-broking-and-asset-management arm had been acquired by a larger stock-broking firm. The shares we had received in the takeover were worthless. In US-dollar terms my shareholding now could not even buy me a pair of Jimmy Choo shoes. So when I say we had a small party for Rudo I mean just that. I am sure Jonasi still had money somewhere. He had to have some stashed away to keep his pretty young thing happy. Lindani looked like she gobbled money for breakfast, lunch and dinner. Just by looking at her you could tell she was extremely high maintenance. You know when she turned up at Rudo's 21st I was trying to figure out who was older, Rudo or her? My poor daughter was so embarrassed that her father had brought his paramour along. I think Trevor (her fiancé) was even more embarrassed for her. Linda, or whatever her name was, pranced around the place like a diva. Everything of hers was over the top from the make-up to the outfit. She had a tiny little black body-hugging dress on so short I could see the stretch marks on her arse. They had tried to have kids but she had miscarried God knows how many times. If you ask me it was a good thing because Jonasi had nothing left to offer to the world.

twenty-two

When Jonasi casually informed me that we were going to Rudo's 21st party I was over the moon. Nowadays we never went anywhere and this business of sitting in the house like geriatrics was making me go ballistic. As I dressed, I could hear him coughing in the bathroom. I could almost see the sputum flying all over and splattering onto the mirrors. He coughed longer than usual.

"Are you alright in there?" I asked.

"I'm fine," he replied brusquely.

Jonasi was far from fine. He was trying to keep it together for my sake acting like everything was under control when I knew things were falling apart. I had seen Jonasi at his best and also at his worst. These past two years his health had deteriorated and I had watched him slowly dissipate in front of my eyes. His illnesses were sporadic but each depleted him. First it had been his bout of TB then he had recovered. Then it was shingles. It was on and off, just like everything else was in our lives nowadays. My biggest misfortune was that I had bought shares in a bear market now I was sitting on a heap of losses in a market that showed no signs of recovery. Jonasi was going down fast like the Titanic and I was sinking with him. You can rest assured I did not want to go down with Jonasi. The good thing is we did not have any kids. Not for lack of trying. I had miscarried Farai's kid in my seventh month. I was devastated. You have no idea how excited I was about having that child and just like that it bailed out on me, forced itself out of me in a bloody rage. I cried for days. I was inconsolable. Poor Jonasi, he was really supportive and sympathetic. I did not waste time falling pregnant again. At that point you have no idea how desperate I was to have Jonasi's child. He was also desperate for us to have a child together. I guess for me, the baby was my pension and for Jonasi he just wanted to prove his mettle. To prove that he still had it in him. But you know what, my womb would not co-operate. My uterus let me down so many times that the doctor just pulled me aside and said I should just leave it be.

"Pregnancy in your state is not a good idea," he said.

"What do you mean?" I challenged him as I lay in bed, IV tubes taped to my hands.

"You are HIV Positive," he replied, "You need to give your body time to regenerate and be strong. Your CD4 count is extremely low and I want to start you on ARV treatment."

I lay there and felt like I had been hit over the head with a sledgehammer. What the hell did he mean I was HIV Positive? The way he said it so casually like we were talking about period pains and tampons. I felt hot all over and surges of panic charged through my body. How could I possibly be HIV Positive? Where in the hell did I get the HIV?

"Does Jonasi know this?" I asked in a panic. "Have you

told him?"

"I haven't spoken to your husband but I think you both need to get tested and start on some course of treatment."

I turned on my side away from the doctor's intent gaze. I was not HIV Positive. It was a mistake. They had probably mixed up my results with someone else's. I have seen people with HIV; they look nothing like me. I am a beautiful woman. Sometimes Jonasi cups my face in his hands and tells me over and over again how beautiful I am. I have an amazing body at the best of times. It's just that with all this pregnancy shit it had been starting to sag but wait until I was out of hospital I'd be fine. I'd show them that I was not sick. Sick people did not look the way I did.

"Look," continued the doctor, "I can speak to your husband if you like. I know this is a difficult subject to broach."

"No it's okay, I'll speak to him," I replied, in a muffled voice.

He left me to cry into the pillow. As much as I wanted to deny it, the writing was on the wall. Our days were numbered. Still I refused to accept it. I was fine. We were both fine. We were both going to be fine. The minute I got out of hospital I whipped myself into shape. I went jogging every morning, Jonasi panting behind me like the tired dog he was. Now that Jonasi had left his wife of 20 years for me he was in my face 24/7. I could not eat, sleep or shit without him knowing about it. You see he would not let me go to the gym because he said he did not want other men seeing me naked. For a very upwardly mobile man Jonasi had some very archaic tendencies. He was intensely possessive over me. Even when I left the house he insisted on knowing where I was going, who I was going with and how long I would be gone for. If I so much as stayed out for longer than anticipated he would start calling me like a nagging wife. Sometimes I would leave my cell phone at home or just switch it off. Look I know Jonasi provided me with security but sometimes I just craved a mind-blowing shag with a man with tight buttocks and a six pack.

Then Jonasi emerged from the bathroom looking haggard. He had lost a lot of weight and was looking rather emaciated, his shrivelled stomach looking like a used condom. Trust me I tried to get him to eat but he did not have much of an appetite for much nowadays. Now you see why I had to go out for a bit of excitement. The sight of him was depressing me.

"Sweetie," I spoke kindly, "aren't you getting dressed?"

"You know what; I'm thinking maybe we shouldn't go. I don't feel too good."

"You are fine Jonasi," I replied dismissively, "and we are going to the party."

"I'm really not feeling up to it."

I threw my hairbrush at him. He ducked and it hit the wall behind him.

"I'm tired of sitting in this fucking house, Jonasi!" I screamed. "Put some clothes on your tired ass. We are going to that party even if it kills you!"

I had never been to Joyce's house before so trust me I was looking forward to it. I was also keen to meet Joyce whom I had only ever heard about. I drove and Jonasi sat in the passenger seat looking like he had constipation, his red, cracked lips drawn in a tight line. I know he was angry with me but I knew he would get over it, he always did.

"Sorry I screamed at you earlier," I spoke, feeling sorry for him.

I put my hand on his bony thigh and stroked him gently. A few years ago that would have fired Jonasi up but he did not even twitch. I gave up trying and focused instead on getting us to the party safely. Joyce's home was massive and inviting. Joyce herself was thin and unreceptive. I now understood why Jonasi had left her. She looked like a frigid cow. Rudo was a carbon copy of her mother. She just overlooked me and smothered her father with kisses. I was later introduced to her fiancé, Trevor. I decided that I would sleep with him for the fun of it. I knew I could. He looked highly strung like he was not getting any anyway. Actually I looked around and there was a dearth of people there. It was just Rudo's girlfriends. Typical uppity suburban girls who thought they were God's gift to mankind. There were a few guys too and all of them seemed like they were spoken for. I helped myself to a Smirnoff Ice in the cooler box and one of the girls gave me a dirty look. I disappeared into the house thinking I would watch television instead. The inside of the house was grander and furnished in the utmost splendour. I decided then that the minute Jonasi and I got married I would also get a bigger house. Assuming he lived that long. I looked at him now and he was such a pathetic sight. Poor Jonasi. All our grand plans had come to nought. I found a young virile-looking man lying topless on the couch watching television, drinking a beer and munching on a braaied piece of sausage.

"The party's outside," he said when I walked in.

"It's a boring party," I replied, throwing myself onto the couch.

I kicked off my high-heel shoes. I was overdressed for the occasion. Maybe I could go clubbing with this hunk of a man. I would drop Jonasi at home and go and dance the night away somewhere. Sometimes I did that when I was stressed, which was very often.

"Who did you come with?" he asked

"Jonasi," I replied.

"What's a pretty thing like you doing wasting yourself on an old man like him?"

"Trust me, I ask myself the same question every day."

We both laughed. He was the only one with a sense of humour. Everyone else in this house was tight assed.

"You don't look like a Smirnoff girl, can I get you a whisky instead?"

I did not refuse and so me and my newfound friend drank and talked. When Jonasi came looking for me he found me with my legs in the air and Garikai thrusting wildly inside me. We were at that point of no return. Jonasi just shut the door and walked away. It was only after I had come that I went rushing outside to look for him. He was sitting stone-faced in his car.

"Are you ready to go home?" he asked me.

"Yes," I replied.

I stole a quick glance at him and could see the tears streaming down his face. We drove home in silence. I was filled with shame. I did not know why I kept doing this to him or myself. Jonasi was really good to me. Look he had done for me what most men had never done. I vowed I would not cheat on him again. That's what I always said until I had my next big itch.

That night we did not sleep. Jonasi coughed all night and stank up the room in the process. When I said the man was in a state of decay I really meant it. Jonasi got much worse after that night. I felt like it was my fault he was ill. I really tried though. I sat by his side nursing him but he was just not getting better. That was the second time he was admitted into hospital. Apparently he had pneumonia. The doctor pronounced what I already knew, Jonasi was HIV positive. He advised him to start on ARV treatment. As he lay shaking under the blankets he agreed. I think at that stage he would have agreed to anything. Jonasi did pick up strength and got well again. He was strong enough to come home and to do the things we had done before. He was very attentive and he took me out more. We even travelled around the country with him playing golf. Then he stopped taking the ARV treatment.

"Jonasi, the doctor said once we start we can't stop," I chided him.

"Screw the doctor, what does he know? I'm not sick. Only fools get HIV."

He flushed his consignment of tablets down the toilet. I carried on taking my medication religiously. Maybe he felt he did not have much to live for but I did. I was still young and beautiful and I was not going out like that. It's funny how you sometimes wish you were dead but when there's a remote possibility that you could be you want to hang onto life with all you've got. However Jonasi had really given up on life. He would drink himself into a stupor. I hated going out with him because when he got drunk he also got increasingly violent. He would beat me and start blaming me for giving him HIV. On some days he would be incredibly sweet and would cry until he fell asleep.

"Sweetie maybe you should go for counselling," I crooned.

"You or me? I think you need it more. You are the one who has a problem keeping your legs shut."

You know I was really trying to be supportive, really trying to keep it together but when he said things like that it made me want to run straight into the arms of another man. Then one day he got extremely sick. He just started vomiting blood and had to be hospitalised. He spent almost three weeks in hospital. It seemed one thing led to another. First it was his legs. He screamed of a constant ache inside his bones. I would sit at his side massaging him. Then it was his head. He cried that the pain in his head would not go away. They kept him in hospital for almost a month and then discharged him saying there was nothing more they could do for him as his HIV had progressed into full-blown Aids. He was in so much pain and there was nothing I could do for him either. He stopped eating and each time we tried to force him it would either end up as vomit on our laps or shit in his underpants. Sometimes I would leave him at home with Grace and go drinking just to get respite from it all but the minute I got home it would be like his illness had intensified. We would not get an ounce of sleep because he would be howling in pain. There was just no way I could escape his anguished cries. Life with Jonasi became increasingly unpredictable. Some days were better than others. He would look like he was getting better than almost overnight he would get worse. I just could not cope. That was when I decided to call Joyce. I knew then I was in over my head in this. This was more than I had bargained for.

twenty-three

You know when I got that call from Lindani I knew the shit had hit the fan. Rudo and I went over to Ballantyne Park to see Jonasi. He looked like a corpse that had escaped from the graveyard. I mean the last time I saw him at the party he was looking really emaciated. I had attributed it to the stress of keeping up with a younger woman. He had aged considerably and was almost bald. You could count the ginger strands of wispy hair sprouting on his pimpled, crabby, peeling head. His skin was dull and lifeless and his complexion the colour of midnight, his red eyes and lips like burning coal.

"What do you want me to do?" I asked Lindani.

She was sobbing hysterically, "I can't cope with this shit! I've tried but I can't."

"So now I'm supposed to cope with the shit is that it?"I shouted back.

Why was it suddenly my problem now that Jonasi was sick and incapacitated?

"He's your husband."

"So now you realise he's my husband?" I shot back. "A

few years ago it didn't bother you! Well you know what? I don't want him."

I was being brutally honest. I did not want Jonasi, especially in the state he was in. I know they said it was for "better or for worse" but you know what, Jonasi had gone hunting for this dreaded disease. Now that he was strung up and near death I had to act like the supportive wife? Hell no, my cheerleading days were over. I had long since retired from that game.

"Mummy please," cried Rudo, "We've got to help Daddy."

"Lindani will take care of him," I replied nonchalantly.

"I can't," sobbed Lindani. "God knows I've tried but I can't do this anymore."

"Please Mummy!" wailed Rudo.

She had tears rolling down her high cheekbones. The thing is Rudo could cry all she liked but at the end of the day the responsibility was mine. I would have to nurse him. I would have to make sure he took his medication. I would have to bathe him and clean after him. I'll be honest with you, I was not up for it. I just did not have the strength. But as much as I wanted to turn and walk away I knew deep down I could not turn my back on him. Even after all the betrayal, lies and animosity he was still the father of my children. So once again I was laden with the burden of taking care of Jonasi. So that's how Jonasi ended up back in my house. You can imagine the horrified looks on the faces of the twins when they saw him limp into the house, holding onto my shoulder. Even Garikai could not mask his shock. I put Jonasi to bed in the guest room downstairs. He looked at me with questioning eyes. The truth was what was the point of carrying him upstairs, then having the burden of having to move him around if we needed to take him to hospital?

The minute he was settled in I called my mother and told her that Jonasi was back home wearing death like a second skin. She came rushing over to witness first-hand how the mighty had fallen. Afterwards she stood by the door shaking her head in disdain.

"He's not going to make it Joyce."

I nodded quietly. Trust me; I knew that better than anyone else. I guess it was time I called Tino to make arrangements to come home. I would also have to call Wonder and Gershom. All my life I had been the party-planning mistress and soon I would be planning my husband's funeral. How sad was that? When I had married Jonasi I had thought we would grow old together and spend our weekends playing with our many grandchildren. All my aspirations were going to be buried with him.

"You need to start asking him about the will and the money whilst he can still talk."

"Mum don't say that."

"Joyce I'm being real. For all you know they might be nothing to bury him with? He has been giving you nothing but shit all this time so don't start going all sanctimonious on me. Make sure you find out everything, and I mean everything."

I nodded sagely. Mum was right. I did not have money to bury Jonasi and all our funeral policies and life policies had come to nought with the scourge of inflation.

"And one more thing, make sure you handle him with gloves, you might just catch something!"

Even as she said this she was dusting herself. I considered getting a nurse, but it was very expensive. Besides Garikai volunteered himself for the role of his ailing dad's chief caretaker.

"Gari," I cautioned softly, "It's hard work. Will you cope?"

"Oh yes," he replied with gusto. "I want to take care of Dad. I'm glad to see him down like this. Now he knows what it feels like to be at the bottom."

I had expected some sort of warmth and empathy, but Garikai had nothing but malice for his father. Still he took care of him. He washed him, brushed his balding head. During the day Garikai would wheel his old man out in the sun and then take him inside when it was getting a little chilly. Garikai fed him and lifted him into the bed at night. I kept my distance. I won't lie and say I was suddenly filled with an overwhelming sense of compassion for Jonasi. It just was not there. However, being back at home seemed to lift his spirits somewhat. The twins would read to him and play at his bedside when they came home from school. I feared the day they would come home and he would be no more. You see every day Jonasi faded before us. Sometimes when I was alone I would cry. It was hard not to. Our story was not supposed to end this way. What was even sadder was that the Lindanis and Matipas of this world were nowhere to be seen when it really counted, when it really mattered. Essie was the only one who seemed to care what became of Jonasi. She called constantly and wanted to see him but I would not let her. Wonder and Gershom tried to plead her case but I was not moved.

"I don't want her in this house," I responded sourly. "Blessing and Sarah can come but I don't want her here."

"Please maiguru," begged Wonder, "let her see him."

"I said no," I replied staunchly.

Essie could see Jonasi at the funeral like the rest of the world. You might think I was being selfish but I wasn't. Look I had shared Jonasi with every other cunt all my life. At least this was the one time I could say I had him to myself and I *was* going to have him to myself. There would be no Essies, Lindanis or Matipas at his bedside.

This was my time.

Jonasi lived longer than any of us expected. He lived to celebrate his 46th birthday with us. I took the afternoon off and cooked a lavish and sumptuous meal even though I knew Jonasi would only eat a quarter of it. Sarah baked him a huge creamy chocolate cake. We sang for him. All his children were there (well the ones he had bothered to disclose) Tino, Sarah, Rudo, Blessing, Gari, Shumi and the twins. In the evening, Jonasi sat at the head of the table and cracked jokes with us. We really had fun. That night I wheeled him off to his room and felt a quiet joy in my heart. I knew Jonasi was going to get better and that things were going to be okay. I had not felt that way in a long time.

"Joyce could you just lie down with me?" he said in his scratchy voice.

So I climbed into bed beside him. He gripped me with his skeletal hand.

"Joyce I'm scared," he said. "I'm going to die and I'm really scared."

The tears were rolling down his gaunt face. I patted him gently.

"You'll be fine, Jonasi," I said.

He died in my arms. I did not hear him go. But when I woke up that morning his body was cold. Just like that he was gone. Even as I went through the motions of preparing for the burial, I kept thinking that Jonasi would wake up and laugh at everyone and say it was just a prank he was playing on us. At other times I thought I was caught up in the middle of a bad dream. A dream I would later wake up from and relate to my mother and Rudo and we all just laugh it off. I thought back to all those times I had fantasised evil things about Jonasi and could not help feeling bad. Funny how I had hated him whilst he lived but now that he was gone I loved him again. That was the irony of life. There was no rewind. Only in my head could I play back the memories, the good ones, even those were tinged with a bitter sweetness. Still I felt a peace come over me that I had never felt. I knew I would never hurt again. Those days following his death were chaotic. My mother was an unwavering pillar of strength. She handled everything with efficacy, running around and taking charge of the funeral arrangements. She was also there to make sure there was always something to eat for those friends and relatives who had descended upon my home like a hailstorm. My mother had an army come in to take charge of the cooking as there was no way we would have coped. It did not cease to amaze me that even through grief people's appetites never abated. We had to serve breakfast, lunch and supper as well at tea at around 10 p.m. as some people kept vigil through the night singing and dancing. People cried, people laughed and people rubbed each other up the wrong way. Half the time I was dizzy with exhaustion, only managing to get a few hours' sleep here and there during the day. Even this was a battle as my home was always teeming with people, their loud voices reverberating around the house. You know I was counting down the days till Jonasi's burial so that this whole circus would come to an end. I would have happily drunk myself into a stupor but you know I had to keep up appearances as the grieving wife. Then you'll never guess who showed up in the midst of it all.

Matipa.

twenty-four

I read about Jonasi's death in the *Sunday Times*. Some journo had written a lovely obituary about him, his life and how he had pioneered a new breed of black technocrats in Zimbabwe. My head was literally spinning when I put the paper down. I could not believe Jonasi was dead.

"What's wrong, honey?"

That was Mark, my husband, sitting across the table from me. We were sitting out on the patio of our New Hampshire home. It was one of those rare occasions in the England summer when you could actually bask out in the sun. I had met Mark five years before on a flight to the United Kingdom. After I had fled from Zimbabwe I had gone to China. I had spent a couple of months playing pussy foot to Mr Guangzhou before deciding what I would do with my life. I know a lot of you think I was a bitch to leave my kids behind but it's not like I left them with strangers; I left them with their father. Don't judge me. I did what I thought was right at the time. Jonasi took care of his own and I was certain my girls would be well taken care of. I knew Joyce was not going to be the stepmother from hell so I slept easier at night knowing they were loved and cherished. The decision to leave them behind had not been an easy one. I carried those girls for nine months before they tore themselves out of me. I know you don't believe me but it broke my heart.

"Mattie what's wrong?" asked Mark in a louder voice.

"My ex is dead," I replied. "Just shocked, it was so sudden and abrupt."

Mark came over and held me in his arms. He is a really sweet, loving guy. I met him on Qatar airlines when I was headed to London and he was connecting from Singapore where he worked as a derivatives trader. Mark said he was attracted by my dark, smouldering looks. You see, whoever said black is not beautiful lied. Mark is the complete opposite of me. He is tall with blonde wavy hair and sea-blue eyes. A very handsome man and you know what, he's all mine and he loves me for me. He knows about my past and he loves me still so what more could you possibly ask for?

"I really think I ought to go to the funeral for my kids' sake."

"Do you want me to come with you?" he asked.

I nodded in the affirmative. Trust me I would need the moral support. Mark is now retired. He dabbles in the stock market from his laptop at home and we travel. We don't have any children. I could not have any even if I tried. (After the twins I had my tubes tied.) Well Mark is not too fussy about kids but more and more I find myself thinking about my girls. I really want to have them here with me. Now that Jonasi is dead I don't think it's fair to leave them with Joyce. I know Mark will understand. It's not that he hates children but our lifestyle so far has not exactly been child friendly.

Mark and I flew out on the first flight we could get to Zimbabwe. I had not been home in over five years and the landscape had changed drastically. Even when Mark and I were married, we had a private ceremony in the Bahamas and we flew my parents over. You know I would talk to my mother over the phone and she would say things were bad but you know I had not realised just how bad they were. Look, there was a recession all over the world but things in Zimbabwe were beyond the recession stage. My mother said things had improved but I could not see it. All I could see was dilapidated infrastructure, unkempt buildings and a country in overall decline. I was ravaged with guilt to think my daughters had been trying to survive in this environment. When I went to see them, they looked happy enough. There was not even a flicker of recognition in their big brown eyes. Now that really broke my heart. I gave them life. You think there would be some eternal bond or iota of emotion but they just clung to Joyce. I had brought them pretty frocks and shoes but they were not moved. I wonder if Joyce had told them stuff about me. You know Joyce was looking like a bitter bitch. Time had really hardened Joyce. She was really cold and aloof. To think we were once close to becoming friends? Now she looked at me like I was the enemy.

"Matipa you couldn't even call or send money all these years?"

"I couldn't," I replied.

She snorted in scorn. You see there was nothing I could say or do to justify my actions. I did not expect Joyce or any of you to understand.

"Look Joyce I'm really thankful for everything you've

done but I want to take the children."

"With my pleasure," she replied archly.

That was easy enough. I had expected some sort of confrontation but I figured Joyce would be happy to be rid of them. However, one glance at the twins and I knew my decision would be met with resistance from them.

The only reason I went to the wake was to try and re-establish a bond with my daughters but they ran away from me. I decided to take them out to Dune Estate for lunch one afternoon. Joyce had dressed them in the pretty matching Jeep frocks I had bought for them and they looked so beautiful and angelic. My heart constricted and I was filled with overwhelming love and guilt for ever leaving them. They both ordered milkshakes, a green one for Ashley and a pink one for Hayley. I was surprised they even knew what a milkshake was. As we waited for our food to arrive we chatted gaily. They were reticent and ill at ease at first. I figured it was because they probably did not get out much. Then it hit me that the death of their father had really affected them when Ashley said to Mark, "Our Daddy died and now our Mommy is sad. Do you want to be our Daddy?"

Mark blushed, "I would love to," he replied with utmost sincerity.

"We love our mommy so much," continued Ashley.

"I'm your mommy," I interjected, "Auntie Joyce was looking after you."

Hayley shook her head vehemently, "You are not our mommy. Our mommy is beautiful."

"And she loves us very, very much," added Ashley,

"She loves us more than anything in the whole wide world," agreed Hayley, demonstrating with her hands just how big Joyce's love for them was.

I could not hold back the tears from rolling down my cheeks. I hated Joyce then. She had usurped my place in their hearts. I had given birth to them and here they were telling me I was not their mother. Mark squeezed my hand and told me to be patient. He said with time I would win them over but I knew deep down they were lost to me forever. And so as people cried for Jonasi during the wake I shed tears for my children. Even at the church they walked in with Joyce's bunch, their tiny hands interlocked with those of Shumi. I wondered if it was appropriate for children that young to be at a funeral but Joyce smirked and said it was. I was seated behind Joyce, though you could not see the madam herself as she was hidden behind a huge Christian Dior hat with black roses. The first three rows had been reserved for close family but I guess that definition could have been stretched to include me. Just as well because we got the best seats in the Lord's house. You see the church was packed to the brim. People were spilling out onto the courtyard and into the street. There had been a lot of pushing and elbowing just to get inside the church. My black Vera Wang dress had almost been creased in the melee, trying to enter the church. I had gone for the understated glamorous look and looked cool behind my Prada sunglasses. My biggest accessory was Mark; he was by my side, holding my hand in his. I spotted Lindani and her mother in the seat across the aisle from us. I had met Lindani during the course of the week prior to the funeral. I had gone to inspect things at my Ballantyne Park home. You can imagine we had an altercation of sorts and the mother threatened to beat me up after I told them I would have them evicted. That was my house. I had paid with my ass for that house. Lindani was dreaming if she thought she would just take what did not belong to her. I would make sure the house issue was resolved before I went back to the UK and it would only be resolved when Lindani was out on the street where she belonged. She was a whore, sitting with her golden brown legs crossed over the other. You could see her big brown eyes were darting everywhere, trying to suss out all the men that looked like they had big wallets. She was so obvious; the type of girl who had an itch that she could not scratch. She was dressed like sex on two legs I tell you. The black dress she wore clung to every curve and barely covered her ass. I had stopped wondering what Jonasi saw in each of us. After Essie you put those kinds of questions to rest. Now Essie was drama on two fat feet. You know the hippopotamus of a woman had charged into church like a raging bull in the middle of the ceremony demanding to be recognised. For almost ten minutes she had a verbal slinging match with Joyce whilst everyone inside the church watched with bated breath. Poor Joyce was trying to keep it together being all high class and polite but Essie would have none of it.

"I have a right to be here!" she screamed, "I have children with Jonasi."

"Essie, I'll have you thrown out," replied Joyce in her high-pitched twang.

"I'll throw *you* out Joyce! You kept me from seeing Jonasi when he was alive but you won't keep me from seeing him now. I'll break your little bony body if you even try!"

I had to stifle a giggle. It was really funny. Joyce would have snapped if Essie even so much as tapped her on the shoulder. She was a big, voracious woman.

"Could somebody get this whore out of here!" called out Joyce.

Essie started to roll up her shirt sleeves. Joyce was going to be bitch slapped. Essie was ghetto through and through and ghetto girls could throw the punches. Just as we were about to witness some action the priest intervened, salvaging what was becoming a rather awkward situation. Mark was insistent on knowing what was being said but you know some things just got lost in translation.

After Essie's little tantrum, the service dragged on interminably, however people could not stop whispering about what had transpired. You could tell no one was really paying attention to the priest but now their eyes were transfixed on Essie. After the sermon, Gershom, Tino and a few business colleagues stood up to give testimonials about Jonasi. However it seemed everyone suddenly had an acclamation about Jonasi that they wanted to share and pushed themselves up to the pulpit. Each had a moving testimonial that transformed him into a saint as people harped on about how Jonasi was a pillar of society, a caring and kind soul who brought immense joy to those around him. Lindani was not to be outdone and took centre stage by giving everyone a complete tribute of how Jonasi had changed her life and how much they had loved each other. Lindani had to be dragged down in a fit of tears. I almost applauded her for that little performance. She had managed to look like the grieving widow and give all the men in the room an unrestrained view of her golden legs in that mini dress. After that, the priest concluded the service with the body viewing. Anyone who was not moved to tears at the sight of Jonasi lying in the casket had to be strong. He was unrecognisable. By the time everyone had filed out of the church there were very few dry faces. The cortège then proceeded to Glen Forest cemetery for the interment.

"Ashes to ashes, dust to dust, we return the body to its original being..."

It was the gravediggers who had the last say as they started to shovel in spades of sand into the grave. Layer by layer the grave was slowly filled up. The older women broke into song, bidding Jonasi his final goodbye. When the grave was finally filled up, wreaths were placed on top. Then his daughters, Rudo and Sarah read out cards and letters of sympathy; a task they failed to do without losing their composure and shedding a tear or two. Wonder came forward and did the vote of thanks and invited everyone back to Joyce's home for lunch. You can bet we were going there. I knew the drama was not over yet and trust me I did not want to hear stories narrated to me by some third party.

twenty-five

Scores of people flocked to Joyce's home to pay their respects. I was one of them. I was not going to be left out. I had every right to be there. I had played a major role in Jonasi's life and I was not going to let anyone, especially Joyce, stop me from going. I had not been an extra, I had been a supporting actress, the best one at that and I deserved an award of recognition. She wanted to act like I had not mattered, well trust me I did matter.

"Mum could you please behave yourself," chided Sarah. "What you did in church was embarrassing!"

"Tell me about it," added Blessing. "I wanted to dig a hole and die."

"Just shut up," I hissed. "You don't know what you are talking about. Besides whose side are you on?"

Sarah did not respond but she had that holier-than-thou look on her face. At 25, Sarah had a mind of her own and that mind said I was in the wrong. She sympathised with Joyce and judged me harshly for being her father's second wife. She did not even look it at that way, she just saw me as a home wrecker.

"I mattered to him!" I sniggered. "He married me of his own will."

"You were fornicating with a married man," she replied.

"Don't judge me!" I hissed, "You have no right to judge me!"

I almost reached out my hand and slapped her across the face. She had no right to talk to me that way. She also had no right to judge me. I had done at the time what I thought was best. Did she think she would be where she was today if it was not for me and everything I had done? We drove all the way to Folyjon in silence. We struggled to find parking in the crescent as flashy cars choked the long winding driveway and spilled out into the street which had to be cordoned off. A stranger who might have walked in could have been forgiven for assuming they were having a party, as immaculately dressed women and men alike lingered on the lawn drinking fine whiskey, expensive wine and beers. Food was being served from a long buffet by uniformed waiters. It was quite ironic that so many people had turned up for Jonasi's funeral yet none of them had really known him in the true sense of the word. You can say what you like but I knew the real Jonasi. I had known him intimately and no one could take that from me. He was only really ever at ease when he was with me. However stepping into Joyce's fiefdom I felt ill at ease. I had never set foot inside Jonasi's house. To call it that was an understatement; they lived in a palace and Joyce was the queen strutting around with airs, commanding servants to do her bidding. She looked the part of the grieving black widow I tell you. From head to toe she was decked out in an expensive Salvatore Ferragamo suit and pointy Ferragamo stilettos. She even wore black lace gloves that revealed perfectly French-manicured hands. The diamonds on her fingers and around her neck glittered to high kingdom come. I really felt like a poor relative from *kumusha*. I felt like I had been living in a backyard shack all my life. Surely if I had meant something to him he would also have built me a mansion? Or at least given me a substantial amount of money to see me through till the end? You know when he passed I never got a cent of Jonasi's money. I knew it was Joyce's doing. She probably forced him to stop supporting me financially because the money-well dried up, I tell you. My life had become extremely difficult. I no longer received a salary. My car was no longer serviced. Jonasi even stopped paying school fees for Blessing. I could not afford to take him to South Africa and so he had eventually enrolled in the University of Zimbabwe. And here was Joyce and her kids living in the lap of luxury when on some nights I had almost gone to bed without food and you know I'm on medication and I can't afford not to eat.

I made my way to the buffet table and started to help myself to some food. I had to take my ARVs religiously. If there's one thing about my daughter is that she knocked some sense into me about my health. She said I could see all the faith healers I liked but I was not to lose sight of the reality that I was HIV positive. And you know what, that hard talking saved me because I was alive and Jonasi was dead. It could have been any of us being buried today but I had chosen to live. If Jonasi had also accepted it he might have been alive today. That is why I had so badly wanted to see him in the end but Joyce would not let anyone get to him. I really hate Joyce. I hate her with all my being. She thinks she's all high and mighty but she's going to die too. We are all going to die in the end.

I was chewing on a chicken drumstick when I was joined by Matipa. I had not seen her in ages and remember thinking that she might have died before all of us but here she was looking all beautiful and happy. We had never really spoken before so I was really surprised when she came up to me and offered her condolences. My eyes misted with tears. No one had even acknowledged me or my grief. I felt pain too you know.

"Have you eaten?" I asked, licking my fingers. "The food is really good."

I was just thinking of how I could get hold of the leftovers. I had already shoved some lamb chops into my handbag. These days I could not even afford a gram of steak. At best we had ration meat.

"I might get something later," she replied. "Need to watch the waistline."

The things some people worry about. Matipa looked like one of those Somalian war victims in a refugee camp. She really needed some flesh on her bones. She was still the ugliest thing I had ever seen with her long black weave that reached her tiny waist. It actually made her look like a witch. I reckon she had bewitched Jonasi to get him even to like her. Girls like Matipa used *muti*. I should know; I've met a number of them when I've gone to see Philemon. They all have the same specs. Their faces are covered in thick layers of Estée Lauder foundation. They batter their fake eyelashes and draw their glossy lips into fake smiles. They like to act like they have a lot of class but deep down they are dirty. Look how else do you explain how a person who looks like Matipa ends up with a handsome white man like the one I saw her with in church? Trust me; whatever *muti* she uses it is potent.

"So where have you been?" I asked her out of curiosity.

"Overseas. I'm married now."

She waved a manicured hand in front of me, showing off a huge rock. I pretended not to notice it even though that diamond was staring me in the face.

"A lot of people get married for papers I hear."

"Not even," she replied quickly. "We love each other."

"Where is he?" I asked tartly.

"Mark went back to the hotel. He said he wouldn't know how to behave."

She was lying. She probably told him to go so that none of the other women would get any ideas of cosying up to him. When you look like Matipa you need to protect your turf. The poor guy probably had never seen any black women before Matipa. The last thing she would do is to expose him to anything remotely better.

"At least you've got a good man to take care of you. Aren't you looking for anyone to clean your house? I could do with a job."

She laughed. She probably thought I was joking but I was serious. I needed a job but she would not have hired me anyway; probably too afraid I would steal her husband. If I were in her shoes I probably would not hire me either. I was just trying my luck. Things were not easy at all. People saw me all round and robust and thought things in my life were fabulous. They were not. The ARVs had made me balloon to tremendous proportions.

"Joyce really gave him a wonderful send off," commented Matipa.

"Did you see the coffin? It must have cost a fortune. They should have given me half the money."

Actually the more I thought about it I figured I would ask Freedom to dig him up and sell the coffin. Chances are we did not make it into the will so we might as well make money out of what's left of Jonasi. Don't scowl. Jonasi is dead, it's not like he can feel anything.

"Joyce really tried," continued Matipa.

"It won't change anything. All this fancy stuff won't raise Jonasi from the dead!"

"How did Jonasi die anyway? I never got to hear."

I was quick to spill the details of Jonasi's death as had been narrated to me by Gershom and Wonder.

"It was HIV. Apparently Jonasi would not take his medication. He refused to believe he was HIV positive!"

Matipa gasped in horror, "How unfortunate hey!"

"It's Lindani who gave us HIV," I said.

"So then Joyce probably has HIV as well," concluded Matipa.

"Trust me the year won't end with Joyce still alive," I remarked. "Just look how thin she is! If she goes on to a scale she probably won't weigh more than 15kg."

I caught an eyeful of Joyce. She was engrossed in a conversation with a rather tall, handsome portly looking man. They looked rather too intimate to me.

"Who's he?" asked Matipa following my gaze.

"I heard them call him Baba Dzenga," I replied. "Apparently he paid for everything. All this food you see. These drinks we are having. It's his money. I mean how many funerals do you attend that are catered for by Holiday Inn?"

"He must be loaded."

"You know I used to think Joyce was a bit dumb but you know what, she's probably been getting it on all this time. I'm sure she gave us Aids. *Zvakaoma asikana.* (It's hard, ladies)."

"Joyce is HIV negative."

We both turned around and we were staring into the eyes of Joyce's mother. She walked off and left us to gossip. What could she do after all? Arrest us? And so the rapport continued and all over the house, similar conversations were taking place, conversations that would surely have raised the dead.

epilogue

I had a beautiful send-off indeed. So beautiful I wanted to come back from the dead and thank Joyce personally. My poor wife had really gone out of her way to give me a hero's departure. The church had been elaborately decorated and the choir sang beautifully. Not even Essie's little tantrum could have deflected from the splendour of the ceremony. Garikai, Blessing and Shumirai had done the readings in church. So eloquent and well spoken, true Gomora men, I was proud. Tinotenda had given a moving testament about me and how he admired me and how I had inspired him. I was really touched. Touched to the core. Even the five-man gun salute at my graveyard had been a spectacular showcase. I really went out with a bang I tell you. Then my little twins had thrown long-stemmed roses onto my coffin before they filled it with sand. And my daughters had read loving tributes to me. You almost wish you could rewind these moments. It had been a magnificent affair. I would not have expected less from Joyce, but it had been beyond my expectations. My dear Joyce, she had been the most beautiful woman there.

So stunning in black. She shone that day, even brighter than the August sun. She had kept up the charade till the curtain of my life had come down. She had good PR, my wife. It beats me why she went and chose a career in accounting instead of marketing. Well I guess that was all Stanslous's influence. I could see him cosying up to her. He's wanted Joyce for a long time and now that I'm dead I'm sure he's going to go after her full force. I know Joyce won't say no. She needs a man to latch onto. Not just any man either. Got to hand it to her, she gets bigger and better. At least she had the integrity to wait till I was dead and buried. Which is more than I can say about my other wives. Lindani was shagging men inside the house whilst I tried to sleep in the next room. She's a noisy lover so I could hear her scream in delight whilst I writhed in pain. She thought I was stupid. Thought I did not realise that she brought men home with her. She would tell them that her sick father was asleep in the bedroom next door. Well I got the last laugh because she did not get a dime from me! She'll have to go and sell her sorry ass to the highest bidder. Maybe I should not be so bitter, we both used each other. For me, I was an old man trying in vain to relive my youth through her. They say life begins at 40; well it would seem mine ended there. I used her to hoist my ego and sometimes my flagging libido. Men envied me when I had her on my arm, which was good because towards the end there was nothing enviable about me. I had lost everything I had worked for. My business had gone down the drain. My family life had followed suit. Even my own kids did not respect me. To top it off, Joyce had stopped loving me. I guess the question on all your tongues is which of my "wives" I loved the most. And most of you are all thinking that it's pretty obvious that I loved

Joyce the most. I didn't. Love is not something you can apportion and put on a scale and weigh. I loved each of my wives for very different reasons. Essie I loved because she was the first woman I ever loved. She was the first woman to show me love and I reciprocated. However I found out the hard way that she would never love me the same way. She tried. Essie was a great pretender and at times I needed that but deep down I knew that it was never going to be. When I went to varsity, girls like Joyce were way out of my league. They were pretty, nice-smelling rich little girls whom I could only have in dreams. But you know what, Joyce walked out of my dreams and into my life. She loved me without my money and believed in me. The combination was potent. And so I worked hard to prove I was worthy. I wanted to be the kind of man she could be proud of. Who could fit into her world and live the kind of life that had never been accessible to me. However it got tiring at times and Essie in the location always reminded me of who I was and where I came from. I could just be me with her. It was never hard work. With her I could just exhale and breathe... I did cheat on them both over the years but it was never anything serious. Mostly one night stands, nothing that could ruffle feathers until I met Matipa. With my legal eagle it was never about the looks. I already had beauty in Joyce and Essie. What I found attractive in Matipa was her brain power. I was used to women who wanted to be taken care of. Women who could only fuck and not even think but Matipa could do both. She stimulated me in a different way but sometimes these brainy broads can become too full of themselves. I don't think Matipa loved me. She loved my money and what it could give her. In the beginning it did not bother me but in the end it did, especially after the twins were born. Joyce was probably the only one who loved me sincerely. But she too stopped loving me in the end. I fell in and out of love with Joyce several times but I never stopped loving her. She was the only consistent thing in my life. She was there through the ups and downs, the ins and outs. She was there to hold my hand in the end. I'll be honest with you, Joyce could never have given me everything I wanted in a woman but which woman ever can? It's true what they say about the 80:20 rule. I had 80 percent at home but tried to satiate the 20 percent elsewhere and ended up with a 120 percent! Look I had it good, better than most men could ever have it but I wonder was it worth it? Look at all the pain and destruction I caused and in the end I didn't even have Joyce's love when I needed it the most. Well I hope Stanslous makes her happy. She deserves to be happy and I've made sure she's well taken care of. I had offshore funds which I entrusted to Joyce before I died. There's no will. I had nothing left to give. Whoever didn't squeeze me whilst I was still alive, to hell with them. I have my very own hell to deal with now. In life you make your bed and you must lie in it; in my case, I'll toss in it!

Lightning Source UK Ltd.
Milton Keynes UK
UKHW010918160522
403010UK00001B/23